Sweet Silver Bells

A Gothic
Holiday
Romance

Elle Kaelee

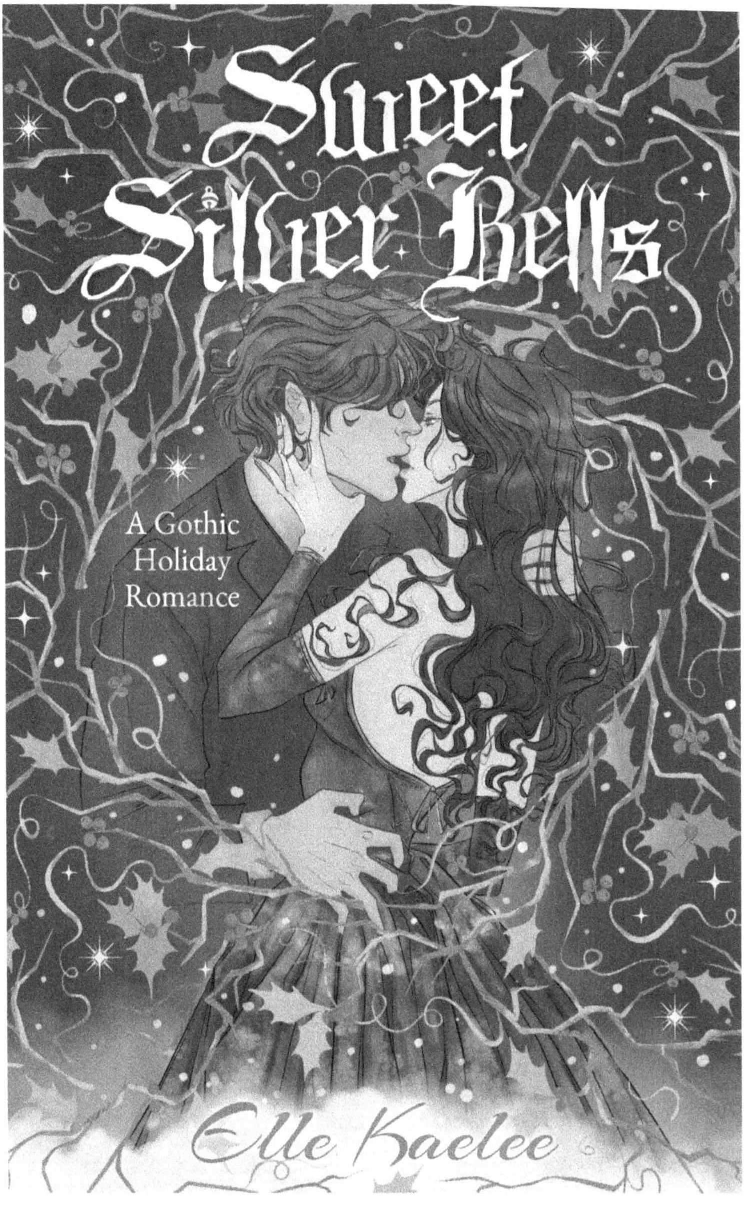

1

CHAPTER ONE.

If there were ever a song of love, a ballad of heartbreak and beauty and strife, it would be the sound of Olivia's voice through the trees. Her song lingered in the forest, the trees absorbing her melodic cries of loneliness and longing. When the magic of the holiday stars glimmer overhead, when the trees sway mightily to music that no one else can hear, Olivia finds herself on the edge of the darkness, looking for retribution, looking for love, looking for a ghost who can find eternity before they disappear together again into the bark.

Outside of Stockbridge, MA | 1914

"Olivia, stop!"

But she did not stop.

Instead, she listened to the sounds of her boots crunching in the snow, cursing the heels that made her move so slowly. He was going to catch her, and she couldn't let him. His life was dependent on it, dependent on her moving, always as far away from them all as possible.

The phantom holy music was there.

It was always there, trying to soothe her, trying to seduce her into the trees.

Today, it would win.

She continued to pump her legs, focusing on not falling over the hem of her gown. The cold stung her lungs as she panted, her heavy breaths blowing warm air—a cloud that followed her, struggling to keep up. She didn't have time to think, to feel—the feeling of knives piercing down her throat while she coughed and gasped.

"These rotten skirts," she cursed under her depleted breath while she worked to peel off her burgundy-stained leather gloves. Her exposed fingers curled as flakes of snow drifted down from the leaves of the dark, ancient trees towering above her.

"Olivia!" a voice shouted behind her.

He was close. She'd hoped he would have given up by now. That he–that they all–would let her disappear.

Don't stop.

Placing her hands on a fallen trunk, she propelled her body over, instantly regretting the gloves abandoned in the snow. They were quickly swept up, though–her father was closing in.

Olivia's skirts ripped, caught on the trunk, the emerald green fabrics embroidered with dark cherry reds trampled. It made it easier to run now; with only two layers of cloth covering her legs she would trip over rocks and brush less often.

She moved as if she were flying, her hands moving to the back of her corset, untying the knot that kept her breaths so short, so painful. The fabric gave way, the bones instantly loosening. Olivia took a deep breath. She could do this. She could get away.

You can't stop moving. You will hurt everyone if you go back.

Tears streamed down her face, her pin-straight, dark-brown hair falling out of the elegant plaits that her mother had spent so long working on. The festive bow had fallen out a long time ago.

"Just stay away," she yelled over her shoulder. "I can't control it. I have to leave."

"Olivia, please." Her father's voice was further away. She was losing him.

You can save him.

Her stomach cramped, her thighs burned, but Olivia did not give in. She was the only one who could protect her family from herself.

A witch.

They had pretended not to know—her mother and father —so politely ignoring the growths, the vitality that responded to her voice, her songs. But time had changed things, and civility was no longer enough. Not now that she had come of age. Not now that it was her first Yule Ball, where she was to meet suitors.

And yet, her stomach still leapt at someone's touch, someone's lingering gaze. A small hope of an everyday life—a small wish for love to find her—fleeting, before it was crushed. Before she revealed herself to everyone who knew her family.

She had almost killed him in front of them all—that boy with wild blue eyes who made her stomach tighten. The boy in the white silk shirt with puffed sleeves, his blond hair slicked back with a single loose curl softening the dimples in his cheeks when he bowed and held out his hand.

Her first dance.

She had moved acceptably, though not exceptionally, eyes downcast, lips tilted in a slight smile, bending into a modest curtsy. Olivia was modest, quiet, and, above all, impeccably dressed. She hardly looked like herself.

She was no longer the girl covered in dirt, running barefoot in the garden, letting soil stain her fingers as she planted her seeds and clipped roses.

No, now she was a woman who had spent hours being bathed, dressed, and styled by her mother and the maids, treated as if she were a living doll.

She supposed that's what being a woman meant: to be looked at, to be wanted—but never glorified. Not like she glorified the moon when it was full and round. Not like when she whispered unknown words and danced immodestly before her window at night, gazing into the forest behind the estate—the forest that had long called to her.

And she hadn't accepted its call—until now.

Until the moment she had to run.

She had to save everyone in that dance hall. They were likely frozen in place. Porcelain cups of champagne spilling down their wrists. Eyes wide. Staring.

You can belong here, she had told herself. The blue-eyed boy had pulled her onto the dance floor.

He belonged there, among beautiful women and wealthy families. They showed off their holiday spirit in ornamental skirts. Their shoes made music of their own. They added rhythm to the six-piece band with perfectly timed, choreographed steps.

The boy spun her. Olivia's steps grew unsure. Then she was in his arms. One of his hands was on her lower back. The other clasped her left.

The butterflies inside her went wild. She had never been this close to someone who looked like him, who smiled like him, who smelled like him. His hand rested low. Her hips were only inches below.

"You are radiant tonight, Olivia," he said. She watched his lips move. She felt the heat of his breath on her neck. The thrill sent a shiver down her spine.

They were dancing. They were touching. Everyone watched. Her mother. Her father. All of them.

It felt illicit.

The thrill surged through her. She smiled so widely that her suitor leaned back slightly.

"I would like to think I could always make you smile like this," he said.

She started to laugh, but she held it in. Emotion was dangerous in polite society.

"When we were all little," he said, "there were stories about you. The wealthy babe who could speak to trees. You sounded like a goddess reborn."

"And do you believe in goddesses?" Olivia asked. The song was coming to an end. Her voice matched the melody of the violin.

"Well, I want to hear you sing," he said, bowing.

"I cannot sing," she replied. Her body froze. Her feet locked in place.

She wasn't supposed to talk about singing. Even the music around them was too close not to feel dangerous—a current she could not afford to fall into.

"Why is that?"

"Because bad things happen." Olivia turned away. She scanned the crowd for her mother, who stood hand in hand with her father. They looked proud, their heads held high, as they presented their daughter to the world.

The band quieted. A small choir of children holding candles marched into the center of the room, still in their cloaks.

"She is a witch!"

It was a cruel joke.

A trap.

A way to mock the outcast.

Olivia's body went rigid. The voice echoed over the hall.

Her hand slipped away from her partner. The dance was over. She turned slowly as the room fell into murmurs and whispers.

The dance hall was enormous, especially to someone as small as Olivia. She had only seen it used a few times before, always for holiday gatherings. A large table stood in the corner, its chocolate and cheese platters untouched—servers glided by with empty trays.

The marble tile gleamed. The ceiling stretched twenty feet above her head. It looked like a place built for royalty.

But Olivia didn't feel royal. She felt ashamed.

"Witch," her dance partner snapped again. His finger pointed to her chest. "The stories are true."

Others gathered around him. They looked like him. Spoke like him. Snickered like him. Their laughter cut through her skin.

"You want me to sing?" Olivia whispered.

Rumors had followed her since she was a baby. Babbling in melodies and making flowers bloom. They would follow her until she died.

The shame twisted into anger. Then resentment came.

They would never accept you. Not this town. Not even if the rumor sounded absurd.

It didn't matter if it was true. It was silly.

You don't believe in silly little stories even if your heart refuses to forget them.

"Olivia, no," her mother said, stepping behind her.

But she couldn't see Olivia's heartbreak. She couldn't feel the anguish rising in her chest. Olivia looked around, searching for something—anything to hold on to. But there was only staring. Boys laughed, and girls her age whispered behind fans and purses.

The Christmas tree stood tall. Sixteen feet of pine filled half the room with the faint scent of sap. It had been chopped down and dressed in ornaments, meant to be looked at. It was not meant to be heard or understood.

How like her it was.

How unjust.

Olivia opened her mouth.

"You wanted me to sing," she whispered. No one heard those words.

But the next sounds from her rose-stained lips weren't heard either.

They were felt.

Cries of horror burst from the crowd as Olivia began to sing.

"Hark, how the bells—"

The dirt beneath the manor was alive. Every root and green thing answered her voice. A crack split the marble tile.

"—sweet silver bells—"

Her voice rose, gathered volume, strength, and power.

The crack widened, splintering across the floor. The Christmas tree responded. Its trunk stretched downward, burrowing through the stone, reconnecting with the earth.

Olivia drew in a deep breath as if she were the tree. It felt as if she were breathing for the first time and had been brought back from an unjust death.

She smiled.

Screams followed.

"Olivia, stop this," her mother pleaded in her ear.

"—all seem to say, throw cares away," Olivia continued singing.

She threw out her arms, and the tree mimicked her. Branches exploded outward, thick and wild, ripping through the marble at every level. Guests stumbled and fell. They ran out of the dance hall and out of the estate.

She spotted the boy she had danced with. He had fallen on the stairs in his escape. He stared up at her, horrified, as if he hadn't believed in witches.

Not really.

Not until now.

"Christmas is here," she sang.

She wouldn't stop. They had seen it. They knew now.

"—bringing good cheer."

"Olivia!"

Her father gripped her shoulder. His face was inches from hers as his eyes pleaded.

The kindness there, the love, had stopped the following lyric from leaving her lips. She shuddered.

Olivia felt ice cold. Her body shook.

She looked around, eyes wide and wild. She only saw ruin and fear. There were people still inside who hadn't managed to escape.

"I told you," said her blond suitor. He stood now, steady on the stairs. His beautiful eyes burned with fury. "She's a witch."

Olivia's hands smoothed the top of her corset. She clutched her skirts and looked down at her feet, weighing what came next.

Because the boy was right.

"Olivia, are you okay?" her father asked.

"Tell Mother I'm sorry," she said through a sob. Tears streamed down her face. Shame burned inside her, but worse than the shame was the hate. The hate for who she was. For what she was.

"Olivia!" her father cried, reaching for her.

But she grabbed her skirts and ran up the stairs and out of the dance hall. Her heels echoed through the foyer.

Guests gasped and froze. Eyes tracked her as if waiting for something, waiting to see what she'd do next.

All she could do was run.

Get away from them all.

Run, Olivia. Run.

"Olivia, stop!" her father shouted again.

The chase began.

Now, in the woods behind the estate, her body screamed. She was exhausted. Her legs dragged, breath ragged.

She knew she couldn't go much farther.

Olivia splashed through a stream, crying out as icy water soaked her ankles. Mud clung to her hem. Snow latched onto her bodice, her shoulders, her hair.

And still, she ran.

Her father was nearly behind her now. The gap between them had almost vanished. She couldn't let him catch her. She couldn't let him hug her, love her, or change her mind. She had to keep him away.

They will be better off without you.

They were better off without the whispers from high society and without the shame of having a daughter no suitor would touch. Olivia would be alone with the flowers, roots, and dirt.

You love the dirt.

Maybe it wouldn't be so bad.

But first, she'd need to sever a few threads of the heart. It would hurt. God, it would hurt. Her parents would heal. They might even have another daughter. Her mother was still young enough.

This is what is best.

She dropped to her knees. Her hands hit the cold ground, pine needles and stones biting into her skin. Olivia turned.

Her father stood there, chest heaving, hands on his thighs as he caught his breath.

"Oh, good God. You've come to your senses," he said, half-laughing.

"If you don't go, I'll have to make you," she said. Her voice shook; even her soul didn't believe her.

His head tilted. The slight smile faded, confusion taking its place.

"I wouldn't just leave you out here, Olivia. You'd freeze."

"Father, go," she said.

A final plea. One last hope.

Please don't make me do this.

"I will not. Not unless you come with me." He stomped a foot into the snow. His chin lifted with that familiar, stubborn pride. He wouldn't yield.

But she wasn't being silly.

"You've left me no choice. Why can't you just go?" Her voice broke. "Leave!"

She sucked in a breath. And then she sang.

I have to protect them, she thought. *I have to protect them from myself.*

"*Hark ... how ... the ... bells,*" she sang, slow and broken. The melody warped, no longer a hymn. No longer holy. It became a curse—a threat.

"Olivia," her father whispered.

With each word, his face collapsed. His pride crumbled. Fear filled his eyes.

"I will not leave you."

She wasn't supposed to sing. She had promised him when she was small. The memory was blurred, filled in by stories her parents had told her. But the promise had been real.

"No," he whispered again. Tears welled in his eyes.

But the earth had already begun to respond.

Her boots trembled against the ground. The dirt shifted, thickened, and churned like quicksand. Branches, snow, and ice moved with it.

"Go," she yelled. Her voice didn't waver this time. "Go!"

The land between them pulsed, crawling toward him.

She could scare him away. She had to try.

It's for his own good.

He shook his head again but stepped back a few more feet.

"*Sweet silver bells,*" she almost yelled. The smoothness of the song crashed against her throat. Cold coated her voice. Tears streaked her cheeks. Fear and pain swallowed her.

This is the only way.

Her father opened his mouth again, but she didn't let his words in.

"All seem to say, throw cares away."

Branches burst from the soft earth between them, thick and dark. The scent of fresh bark filled the air. It gave Olivia some comfort, just enough to hold her focus.

She closed her eyes. She couldn't watch.

The ground shifted again. Branches cracked, stretched, and grew.

He'll run, she thought. *He'll go.*

"Christmas is here, bringing good cheer."

But then a shout tore through her focus. The trance shattered.

She listened for his breath. For his retreating steps.

But she didn't hear them.

He left, she told herself. *He yelled goodbye. He went.*

She opened her eyes.

Branches and vines coiled around her legs. They lifted her and wrapped her. It felt like protection, like armor.

She was a warrior. The forest was her army.

A gurgle snapped her attention forward.

It came from the one person she had hoped and prayed wouldn't be there.

The one who still was.

She gasped.

Her father stood wrapped in vines. But not like she was. Not like armor.

It was an execution—a guillotine.

The forest had risen around him. Branches curled tightly. Thorns, wet from snow, cut through his jacket. Red bloomed beneath the fabric.

A single vine slid up his chest.

Wrapped around his neck.

I can't stop this.

She didn't know how.

She wasn't singing anymore.

"Stop. Please stop," she begged.

But the vines had made up their mind.

"Father!" she cried. She threw her arms toward him.

Fight. Please, fight.

He was bound too tightly.

The vines climbed higher. Thorns slashed his face. Forced his mouth open. His eyes widened. His gurgles were low. He choked.

Olivia could hear her heart shatter. Her father's skin turned white, then red, then gray.

He suffocated.

I murdered him.

The branches didn't stop. They arched up over his head until she couldn't see him at all.

He was gone and hidden inside. The forest had claimed him.

Her breath came in gasps, fast and shallow. She nearly collapsed.

It was done. The very thing she had tried to prevent.

Her mother would never know what happened to either of them. Olivia would never face her again.

Grief surged. A sob broke free. Then a wail.

A sound she had never made before. Deep and raw, a siren's song. A witch's mourning.

Her song.

It rippled around her. The forest responded. Trees grew taller. The moon vanished behind their limbs.

What Olivia didn't know was that sound traveled.

Miles away, her mother stopped along with the guests still

around her. Eyes glazed and thoughts disappeared. Their still bodies moved, the song luring them.

Olivia's wail ended. Their thoughts returned, and hundreds of people blinked. They were confused and all facing the same direction.

Like her father, vines surged around Olivia as she caved into herself, arms wrapping into a hug. The vines did not attack; they did not grow to kill. They grew to keep.

The forest encased her in bark and root. Her sorrow and song transformed into her tree.

She was safe.

Her mother would be safe, too.

As long as Olivia never left the forest, no one else would be harmed.

2

CHAPTER TWO.

Present Day

A hiss in the air, followed by the jarring screech of squeaky brakes, announced their arrival.

"Alright, everyone off the bus," Hunter shouted, standing at the front of the vehicle, close enough to the driver to hear him breathe. Hunter didn't care too much for tight spaces, but what he cared about was often overlooked. With the swinging door open and the cold rushing in, Hunter waved the students off the vehicle.

"Thank God for parent volunteers, am I right?" Sadie, the only other fifth-grade teacher, bounced up smiling. She was the wittiest, least serious person he knew. Fifteen years his senior, she'd declared herself his cool, hip aunt. He needed her dry humor in his life. Otherwise, he would drown alone in a sea of depression. Their school was underfunded, and the fifty-seven kids between their two classes were proof of it.

Sadie fluffed her silver-gray bangs and pulled her long

pigtails down over her shoulders just as a group of boys ran straight into her petite frame, roughhousing as they followed the line outside into the parking lot.

"How many more days until the holiday break?" she huffed.

"Two days. Getting too old for this finally?" he asked, winking.

"Never." She tossed her hair back like a high school girl trying to flirt. "You're one to talk—are you in your fifties yet?"

"I just turned forty and am holding onto that youth for as long as I can," Hunter joked.

"Just don't buy a motorcycle. You might be too old for a midlife crisis. That's for cute little men who just turned thirty-five."

"Oh no, no, I'm far too practical. Besides, I already bought helicopter flying lessons last week."

"God, I hope you're kidding."

"I am," he said after a long pause, as Sadie hit him lightly in the shoulder. "But I probably should. The only people that survive in zombie apocalypse movies are the ones that have access to helicopters."

"Solid logic, Mr. Gunnan. Good to know that you're shaping the minds of our youth."

Hunter smirked and then followed Sadie off the bus. A group of feral kids ran wild, excited and hyped up on the candy canes given out at every store, every library, every grandmother's house around Stockbridge.

When did Christmas blend with Halloween?

The wind at the edge of the manor grounds was sharp enough to slice. It moved through the Berkshire hills in hollow gusts, rattling the bare branches like bones knocking in warning. Snow spiraled, restless and dry.

There was no sun, only a dim, silvery glow pressing through the fog, casting the old manor in shades of sorrow and sleep.

The children's breath curled in the air like ghosts as they chased each other on the asphalt, boots crunching on the frost-hardened ground. The manor loomed above them, its chimneys exhaling faint streams of smoke.

Hunter gave Sadie a look meant to say, *"We will survive this field trip.*

"Alright, students, parents," Sadie shouted, clapping her hands. "I almost have tenure, so let's keep me employed a little longer by making sure no one gets lost. Everyone picks a buddy and then picks a parent. That is your group. Parents, keep track of your groups, and we will all get out of here alive."

"Is she always so severe?" a snarky blonde mom laughed from behind the group of kids.

"Find out whose parent that is and torment them for the rest of the year," Sadie whispered to Hunter. He rolled his eyes, crossing his arms over his burgundy sweater and heavy winter jacket.

"Hello, students of Stockbridge Elementary," a too-perky male tour guide yelled, emerging from behind the buses. "This is Vultauge Manor, built before the Gilded Age. There's a lot of history to explore here, and it's Christmastime, so some carolers are singing in the foyer. Let's go learn."

As Hunter expected, not a single kid seemed impressed or excited. Most of them had their eyes glued to their phones, and he honestly didn't care. He was becoming as bad as the kids, thankful for each day crossed off the calendar as winter break crept closer. He'd rather be alone to wallow in the depression that had clouded him for so long that it now felt like a familiar friend.

That was another problem with this career choice. It required him to be present when staring at a white wall, on a heavy dose of antidepressants, was a more appropriate setting for him. This manor had a bad habit of plunging him into that darkness. It held too many memories.

Their group climbed the path toward the large red-brick manor, surrounded by meticulously maintained grounds. The Berkshires loomed in the near distance, dense with a forest of haunting trees. Hunter always thought those woods looked like they were begging for attention.

There were many stories about the trees, how they were said to be alive with spirits. He remembered being dared as a kid to run through them but never having the nerve. He was made fun of the entire bus ride home, despite no one else running through them either. It was too dark in there, too separated from the sky, the leaves whispering secrets into the wind.

Along the winding path leading to the front steps, lanterns had been lit—too many to be practical. Their golden light bled into the fog, flickering over freshly cleared walkways and wreaths that groundsmen were actively decorating. The hedgerows were trimmed, and the statues dusted clean of snow. Even the great fountain, long dry and cracked, now glistened with a sheet of ice, its edges ringed in evergreen.

"We really do the same field trips every year, don't we?" he mumbled.

"Well, anything else would take effort, and who has time for that?" Sadie laughed.

"Miss Rothlin, I need to go to the bathroom," one of Sadie's students said, twirling her hair nervously as they walked up to the entrance. "My group parent told me to ask you."

"See, what did I tell you? Those parents are useless," she grumbled near Hunter's ear, and he grimaced because there was no way the girl hadn't heard.

"There is a bathroom right when we go inside, in the lobby, up these steps," Hunter said.

"You've been here too many times," Sadie smiled, an edge of sadness lingering at the corners of her mouth. He hated that lingering sadness. It had become unbearable over the years.

"Once a year for every school field trip when I was a mere lad," Hunter said in a terrible Scottish accent.

"That's not all," Sadie said as they followed the back of the group into the front entrance of the manor.

"No. That's not all." There was a cloud that hung over his head that day, and no matter how often he tried to shake it, it was still there. Hunter supposed that time didn't really heal all, no matter how long it had been. Not when he couldn't stand the sympathy that lingered like an oversensitive switch when someone came within ten feet of him.

"Alright, everyone, come inside, gather close," their tour guide said. He looked closer to Sadie's age. Retirees often volunteered within the local historical societies. "Now, Vultauge Manor has been around since 1901. Its original builders were a young couple who excelled in the arts. If I understand correctly, the male head of the household was a writer, although he wrote under a pen name that was never verified to be his true identity. He disappeared alongside his daughter around 1915, leaving his wife to run the manor. It was eventually sold to the state to preserve its historical value. Now, Vultauge Manor is used for field trips and events like weddings and holiday balls."

Hunter tensed, triggered by the introduction. He would never learn to cope.

"Now, everyone, hold your questions until the end. We will begin by touring the interior, followed by lunch on the exterior grounds, before we go in-depth into the gardens."

"Can we go into the forests?" a kid shouted.

"Again, hold all questions until the end—and no, please stay on the grounds with your assigned groups."

"He's a pro," Sadie said. "See? Easy day. I have a bag of sweets in my pocket. I'll be sucking on those and letting my mind wander all day."

Hunter raised his eyebrows at her.

"What?" she laughed. "It's Christmastime, and everyone is doing great."

"You're a national treasure, Sadie. I just want to make sure you get that tenure," Hunter said as their group started to move past the lobby. A gift shop on their right attracted a few straggling kids. Hunter saw Sadie's blonde student emerge from the bathroom. Everyone seemed accounted for.

So far, so good.

"Here, cherry. Your favorite." Sadie held out a hard candy. Hunter sighed and took it, popping it into his mouth right away, the sugar bursting against his tongue.

"Stress eating. I recommend it," she laughed.

Hunter nodded, smiling, his shoulders relaxing just a bit.

They spent the next ninety minutes following the guide through rooms where vintage furniture was roped off and tapestries from a century ago decorated the walls, hanging from the top moldings. Hunter watched as some students' eyes glazed over while parents hushed others whispering through the told histories.

"You know, this place is very brown. I can't remember—was your wedding this brown?" Sadie asked as they entered the last common room—the event space, a ballroom where Hunter had once held a woman in a white dress against him.

His throat dried every time he walked in there. His late wife was a lovely, spritely thing who had insisted they marry right where they met—on this school field trip. Hunter had been in the fourth grade. She'd been in the sixth.

"We had poppies in every color," Hunter said.

"Oh yes, yes, I do remember all the flowers. It did combat the brown." Sadie sighed. "I miss Sarah. She had those eyes that somehow saw your strengths and ignored everything else."

It was true.

Sarah was the only person who had ever made Hunter feel like he was enough. Not for his job, or his potential, but just as he was. Their romance had kindled the summer he came home from college with a degree and a head full of questions.

He'd been nursing a beer alone at the corner of McAllister's bar, wondering if teaching elementary school English was a noble calling or a slow descent into mediocrity.

"Hey, stranger." A familiar voice, low but amused, had cut through the background buzz.

Hunter had looked up and nearly choked on his drink.

He'd known that smile.

"Sarah?" He'd blinked, stunned. "It's been ... what, four years?"

"Five," she'd said, sliding onto the stool beside him like she belonged there. "You look like someone who's about to make a questionable life decision."

He'd given a sheepish laugh. "I might be. I just graduated last year. Now I'm stuck between a teaching job and a quarter-life crisis."

"Well, if you're going to spiral, at least have the courtesy to do it with better beer." She'd signaled the bartender and given him a nod. "Put it on my tab."

"Look at you, all successful and generous. What are you up to now?"

"I'm working over at Siesic as a food scientist. Which is just a fancy way of saying I make sure your granola bars don't kill you."

He'd grinned. "Heroic."

"I try." She'd studied him for a second, more thoughtfully. "I always thought you'd end up doing something that mattered. I'm not surprised."

The compliment had landed deep.

"Call me if you decide you need a sugar momma," she'd added with a wink. "I still owe you a drink anyway."

He'd watched her walk away, stunned by how effortless it still was between them.

"She's got you spun, honey," the bartender had said, sliding the new drink toward him. "Want another, or just gonna sit there smiling like a fool?"

Hunter hadn't answered. He'd just looked at the glass, then at the door she'd walked through. He would call her the next night. They'd talk for hours.

Ten years later, he would stand in the same ballroom where they'd had their first dance as husband and wife. Now, he stood beside Sadie and a roomful of students, not the woman who once lit his entire world.

"Are you going to be okay?" Sadie asked.

Hunter knew his face had dropped. He knew tears welled beneath his eyelashes. He knew his fists were clenched.

"I think a lot of women like a man who can cry," Sadie said. "I'd use it."

"Sadie, it would be completely appropriate for you to give me some space," Hunter said.

"Sure thing, man," she said, slapping him on the shoulder.

"How come you guys can talk during the tour, but we can't?" asked a boy with combed-over chestnut hair that hung down to his chin like he had just been to Warped Tour.

"You might make a good lawyer someday, Brandon," Sadie said. "But ultimately, the answer is because we said so."

"And that's it for the inside," the tour guide announced, clapping his hands. "Now I think we will take lunch outside and rejoin for the garden tour in about forty-five minutes. Does that work well, teachers and parents?"

"It does," Hunter responded.

"Make sure not to venture into the woods," the guide warned. "That would be an issue for the insurance. All over my head."

"What's out there?" A gaggle of excited students immediately took the bait.

"Rumor has it they're haunted. That if you venture deep

enough into the woods, and you sing, you will wake something terrifying." The guide bent his knees dramatically, holding out his hand like a claw, growing more animated.

"I've sung in those woods on a dare," Hunter whispered to Sadie. "You know, as a kid."

That was a lie.

Why would you lie about that?

"You're such a rebel." She rolled her eyes.

"No, but seriously, they are dense, and it's too easy to get lost," the tour guide continued. "If you go through the back door of the ballroom, it will lead you right back out to a large area of grass. Please bring your trash with you until you can find a dedicated dumpster."

Hunter and Sadie helped push the students to the back and out through the door. The shining sun peeked out against graying clouds, and snow was going to fall by the end of the day. Small bursts of wind caressed his cheeks as he pulled his hood up and grabbed the gloves from his jacket pocket.

"I'm sorry if I was out of line," Sadie said, stepping beside him. "I wouldn't want anything to ruin the professional dynamic we have."

Hunter laughed, which turned into a cough from the freezing air.

"Oh, Sadie, you're the only thing keeping me at this school."

Hunter gazed out at all the students standing on the grass, some nibbling on sad-looking almond butter and jelly sandwiches, but most just angrily staring around with their arms crossed.

That wasn't a lie. He was one bad day away from rotting in his house and never leaving it again. At least he still had a best friend, however crazy she might be, to remind him that he was human.

"I love this stage, don't you?" Sadie asked. "Half of them are too cool to sit down, the other half too practical—'that grass is wet.' How have they not figured out a better place to stuff us for eating?"

"Mr. Gunnan?"

Hunter looked up. One of the boys from his class was angrily marching toward him, his earmuffs pressed tight against his puffed cheeks.

"What's wrong, Killian?"

"Jake dared Levi to run into the forest, and Hudson and Wesley ran after him."

Hunter looked up to the sky and let out a breath.

"This feels like your area of expertise." Sadie laughed. "You know, that inner rebel you have."

"Mr. Gunnan isn't a rebel," Killian interjected. "He's a teacher."

"Wow," Sadie said, trying to suppress a laugh. "You are so right."

"I'll go. Which way?" Hunter sighed.

"Will they get a demerit? Don't tell them I snitched!"

"I didn't know your generation said the word *snitch*," Sadie said.

"My mom's been making me watch her favorite movies from when she was a kid."

"Rad."

"Yeah, that's in them too," Killian said, sighing and turning toward the woods. He pointed in a direction that was still too vague, but Hunter reluctantly walked forward anyway.

"Anyone want to help?" he asked over his shoulder. "No one?"

No one answered, but he did manage to get a couple of dirty looks from a group of girls shivering in the cold.

Hunter stepped out of the overcast light and under the first thick cluster of trees, where the sky disappeared entirely. The smell of cedar and fresh dirt was overwhelming, like walking into a real-life candle store.

"Guys," Hunter yelled, cupping his hands around his mouth. It was silent except for the faint voices drifting in from the manor grounds. These boys were absolutely going to get a demerit.

He wandered deeper, stepping on crunching branches and sticks, through leaves that had fallen and crumpled, brown and withered.

"Levi," Hunter called again. "Hudson."

No one came. No one jumped out to scare him. No one yelled for help from afar.

Hunter checked his watch, deciding they must have returned already. Lunch period was almost over, and clearly, the only one lost in the Berkshires was himself.

He turned around.

Splash.

His boot sank into a shallow creek he didn't remember crossing. The realization hit: he had no idea which direction led back to the manor.

He didn't think he'd gone far, but he'd been searching for a solid ten minutes, according to the classic gold watch strapped to his wrist, a gift from Sarah, one he never took off even after it stopped working. The battery was never replaced. The clock hand would never move again, just as Sarah would never live again.

The forest grew darker as he moved.

Not a good sign.

Hunter pulled out his phone and saw a single bar of service. He kissed the screen and opened the map app, watching as the navigation arrow slowly turned.

He'd be fine. He wasn't as far in as he thought. And if those students weren't lost, their parents would be forced to sit down for a very uncomfortable one-on-one right before holiday break.

Shadows shifted while branches swayed, and a cold, unforgiving wind slapped against Hunter's face.

His entire body shivered.

Crack.

Hunter jumped. His heart rate doubled at the sound of a twig snapping.

"Hudson?" he shouted.

No answer. No footsteps. No voice.

Maybe it was a bird.

Or maybe you imagined it.

Still, as he followed the app's arrow, he let out a hum. His voice made no specific tune, just a low, steady vibration in his chest. The sound comforted him. His shoulders relaxed a bit as he stepped forward, hearing the stream up ahead that he'd crossed before. Recognizing landmarks was a relief. He was headed in the right direction.

His hum grew louder, eventually shifting into casual singing. It was the only thing keeping the creeping unease from crawling up his spine.

"Silent night, holy night."

But then his body froze.

The song stopped.

He'd heard something again. This time, he knew he hadn't made it up.

Something was there.

CHAPTER THREE.

"Hello?" Hunter called out. "I can hear you. Who's there?"

The dense trees above him shed snow that melted and seeped into his cotton gloves. His hands began to ache, the joints in his fingers tight and cracking. Winter was severe, unforgiving.

He had heard another crack, too sharp and sudden for a squirrel or small critter.

"You're getting too far into your head," Hunter muttered, before he went down on the ground, tripping over a collection of roots that were raised just enough to catch his foot. His hand scraped against a tree branch, sending crunching leaves flying and creating a sway in the vegetation above his head. A flurry of wings burst overhead, followed by the angry caws of the ravens he'd disturbed.

Hunter jumped to his feet, adrenaline rushing through him as he kept his eyes down at the glowing map on his phone. He stepped over the creek and kept going, slightly out of breath.

The boys went back. They circled around you somehow.

When he finally stepped out of the trees, he realized he'd

gotten completely turned around, now on the opposite side of the manor.

He stared up at the building, perfectly curated, the brick darker, hidden in a winter shadow. Barren rose bushes with threatening thorns formed a fence, a barrier.

Sarah had loved those rose bushes. She used to gush over them in summer, shooing people away if they tried to pick one. "Let them grow," she'd say. "They want to be beautiful."

Hunter knew the group was likely near the back gardens. He shivered and began walking, his boots squelching in the wet, muddy grass.

"Mr. Gunnam," Sadie shouted as he came around the corner. "I was about to send security to find you."

Hunter walked up to the fence, tall black metal poles connected to a decorated, pointed top.

"Walk around; the entrance is just over there," Sadie pointed.

"Did the boys come back?" he asked.

"Boys?" Sadie blinked.

"The ones I went after."

"Yeah, those boys never even went in. They jumped out from behind a gargoyle or something and scared a group of girls."

Hunter clenched his jaw.

"Of course," he muttered, throwing his hands up. "You really should pay attention to these tours more. There are no gargoyles."

"Whatever it was, it was ugly," she said.

Hunter watched the group behind her move further away, crossing a particularly run-down-looking fountain.

"Uh oh, on the move again," she said, pointing behind her with her thumbs. "Let's go, teach. You ditching students now?"

Hunter marched around the fence, finding the gate.

This garden used to be filled with life and color; he had

photos of it with her in it. He'd worn a deep blue suit and a brown tie and had been made to press his lips to the underside of Sarah's jaw in that pose.

When she laughed, he was supposed to throw her veil behind her to create more movement in the picture. He had to hold his lips there, to her skin, and he tickled her with his stubble for several minutes, the photographer's camera clicking at a rapid pace.

He kept that picture on his desk at the school, framed in gold. Their smiles were both infectious. A year after her death, however, he'd put the photo in the second drawer. It was still there, untouched. That drawer never opened.

Hunter's heart was somewhere else, with someone else. He had resigned himself never to recover, living as a ghost of his former self. He drifted behind the group, his laughter and smile forced, still tangled in a past he hadn't moved on from.

The natural light of the day was already fading as he ushered kids and volunteers back on the buses. He sat in the front this time, Sadie next to him, taking out her crochet the moment she saw him pull out a book.

Safety announcements were made, and the bus drove on until they were back at the elementary school parking lot thirty-seven minutes later. The moment the doors folded open, the kids burst out, feral with freedom.

"Well, I'll see you tomorrow," Sadie said. "Do you need anything?"

"Need anything?" Hunter smiled.

"Oh, you know, you seemed sad. I'm just trying not to be a terrible person."

Hunter shook his head.

"Thanks, Sadie, I'll see you tomorrow."

With that, he stepped off the bus and unlocked his car, his dark blue sedan chirping from across the staff lot. Hunter pushed his hair back and habitually held his hand up to his face to check the time, and that was when he froze.

His watch wasn't around his wrist. His watch was gone. The watch that Sarah gave him.

Hunter's heart sank, guilt drowning him, panic rising in his chest. He couldn't lose that watch. That watch was supposed to stay, just like she was supposed to stay.

Hunter got in his car, turned on the engine, and stared out the window at the excited faces, freed from the public school system for the day. He needed to retrace his steps. He should run back to the bus.

Had he lost it on the bus? Outside on the lawn?

That moment when he tripped in the forest—that had to be it. It was sitting in the dirt and debris, or hanging off a bush or a branch.

Hunter nursed the scrape on the inside of his forearm. It didn't matter if it was dark or cold. He would search all night, and he wouldn't stop until security threatened to have him arrested.

He sped off back into the cold.

It was silent, aside from the gentle hum of the engine, the windshield wipers sweeping in their slowest setting as drops of rain softly tapped on the glass. He didn't focus on the road. Instead, he saw the police officer knocking on the small see-through pane on his classroom door. He saw his hand pressing it open; the man staring back at him with a grim look on his face.

The principal was standing behind him, hands in his tweed pockets, as the officer took off his cap, holding it against his chest.

"Hunter Gunman," he said, "there has been an accident at your wife's lab."

Pulling out of the memory, Hunter turned into the dark, mostly empty parking lot of the manor. He slammed the car door behind him, the sound too loud in the silence. Birds nearby flew into the air at the shocking thud.

The daylight was completely gone, and Hunter moved up the pathway, tripping on the ascending steps to the grounds. He pulled out his phone, using the flashlight to illuminate the frosted-over grass under his boots as he walked around the estate, past the red brick that now haunted him with the memory of love, of what used to be.

He would live with that because it meant he'd been able to know Sarah, hear her dreams, and learn what made her laugh. He'd loved her laugh; it rang through his memories, so light and beautiful. He didn't think there could ever be a sound more capable of cracking him open.

Hunter walked into the trees wrapped in pitch black, a darkness that he imagined rivaled hell. He was desperate, unwilling to relent. He would not give up despite the unease that flitted through him, his throat suddenly dry, knowing that he was a moving target with his light.

There was nothing in these trees. This forest was completely uninhabitable unless you were a squirrel or a bird.

Hunter kept his head down, light shining from his phone in hopes of catching his watch glimmering. He couldn't imagine that he'd miss it; it would be too obvious, stick out too much. Branches twisted against the blackness that haunted his soul, swirling around him like a vortex of nightmares, disorienting him, though he tried to walk the same path he had when searching for those students.

Whatever he'd heard earlier, it hadn't been the boys. It hadn't been anything explainable.

There is no one here, he reminded himself.

There is no one here.

Fallen leaves on top of frosted dirt and dying grass were the only things that gleamed in the light. He continued to move forward, wishing he could see the sky, thinking that the light of the moon, even covered by thick clouds, would be as bright as a spotlight compared to the abyss that welcomed him, and promised to consume him.

You're not looking hard enough. Focus on the ground.

His boots splashed as he accidentally stepped right into the creek, too lost in his head to hear the sound of the gentle movement of the water. He'd fallen right around here somewhere; his watch had to be right nearby. He felt something flicker, recognition, maybe even hope.

Hunter bent down, shoveling around anything movable on the ground around him, studying branches off of bare bushes that were at his eye level and below, still nothing. He was empty-handed, but he wouldn't stay that way. He would find the watch.

You have to find it for Sarah.

He couldn't let it go. He couldn't let her go. That version of himself, when he was with her, was someone else long gone. Now, he didn't know who to be, or what version of himself still existed.

Hunter moved past the creek, now unsure which side he had fallen on. Either way, there was no glint of gold in his light.

The light on his phone flashed, and Hunter's stomach dropped.

"Fuck, fuck, fuck," he said, pulling the device up to his face as the screen turned black, an empty red battery sign flashing before the device turned off entirely, leaving him in lost in the Berkshires, lost in a special kind of darkness that promised never to let go, to wrap him and envelop him so entirely that it wouldn't matter what type of grief or loss he would endure.

You shouldn't have come.

He had followed his heart, and his heart had promised him to a world that seemed intent on eating him alive, never letting him go.

His parents, coworkers, and neighbors would always

wonder what had happened to him, why he had disappeared. If his car were found, would they even bother to come this deep into the trees? Would they look for him as long as he'd been looking for his watch?

He doubted it.

No one was that passionate about him other than maybe his mom. He was an average guy.

Hunter kept his hands and his fingers to the ground. If he was lost to the darkness, he might as well keep searching. If he turned around now, who knew what direction he would wander off in, especially when everything looked the same. Everything was a world of secrets and shadows, waiting for him to hold his breath before it was taken straight from his body.

Hunter kept looking and walking. It was all he could do. He had the stream for reference, but he hadn't come across it again, which made him suspicious that he was lost, too far in. He tried to push away the fear of being trapped there all night, in the cold that was deadly on its own as the temperature plunged. The sun had just set, and there would be too many hours before someone would find his car, before someone might step into the trees and hear him yell for help.

No, they wouldn't hear him yell for help.

You are not leaving without that watch. You are not leaving her here.

There was another crack in the distance, a violent promise in the middle of the silent abyss.

Hunter's breath hitched, and his heartbeat doubled.

There is no one there. Your mind is playing tricks on you.

That could be true.

But then he heard it again.

The warmth of his breath, panicked through his lips, created steam clouds around him. It felt like watching his life leaving him, running away, no longer choosing to stay.

Hunter bent down, sitting on the back of his jacket, hoping

that the waterproofing worked better than he knew it would for a knock-off brand that he could afford with his teacher's salary. He tucked his legs into his sides, arms on his knees, head down in between his legs, and shivered.

"I am a broken man without you, Sarah," he said to himself. "And I've lost more pieces of you. Every day, I seem to have less of you to hang on to."

The trees above seemed to absorb his grief, his cries, and his tears, somehow silent, his words barely a whisper. It didn't feel right, though.

It didn't feel right to be scared. It didn't feel right to be silent.

Hunter lifted his head, a loud sob bellowing from deep in his core.

"I'm sorry," he said to the trees, but he was talking to Sarah. "I'm so sorry I didn't get to come with you. I'm so sorry that I am here and you are not."

Hunter, plagued with grief and adrenaline, was sure that someone was listening, convinced that the cracks he heard in the distance were both a figment of his imagination and really there. Fear itself was summoning it.

He did the only thing he could think of to break the silence, to stop the fear; he started to hum. Low and raw, the sound of his voice wrapped itself around the trees, a barrier, a cocoon of safety because anything malicious or vengeful could not enter through. His breaths slowed and his body calmed as Hunter was enveloped by the cold.

His hum eventually turned into a song in an attempt to comfort himself, to calm his nerves.

"*City sidewalks, busy sidewalks,*" he sang, voice cracking as tears spilled freely. Images of Sarah flashed through his mind, from the Christmases that they had spent together, decorating the tree.

"Can you put me on your shoulders?" Sarah yelled to him from the kitchen.

Hunter stopped cutting the potatoes for dinner and came out into the living room.

"Questions like that are alarming, you know." He smiled.

"I just can't reach the top of the tree." She laughed, holding out a bright gold, glittering star. "I'm just a little baby."

"I've got something you can lift later," he said, his voice low and seductive.

"You think your pickup lines would get better with age." She sighed. "But I think you peaked years ago."

Hunter growled before he dove under Sarah's legs and stood. She screamed and then playfully slapped him on the side of the head a few times.

"Give a girl some warning." She laughed as he stepped closer to their noble fir Christmas tree. She had a habit of breaking off little tufts of needles and pressing them to his nose.

"Smell this. Is there a better smell in the world?"

At that moment, he was between her thighs, so he felt that the question was unfair.

Another branch cracked, this time unmistakably, taking Hunter out of the comfort of his past home life and bringing him back to reality. It was so close, like it was right behind him.

"Hello?" he called out. "Who's there? I can hear you."

But there was no answer.

There was no noise.

There was nothing but the darkness pressing tighter with every breath.

"*Silver bells,*" he sang, terrified, tears welling in his eyes. "*It's Christmastime, in the city.*"

Crack.

Hunter jolted up and got to his feet. It was right behind him.

He turned, trying to make out what was there in the dark,

but all he could gather was an enormous tree, its branches twisted and wrapped around it. Moss protected its bark like a cocoon.

"Is someone behind that tree?"

Nothing.

I'm going crazy, he thought. *It's time for me to resign and become a forty-year-old man who moves in with his parents.*

A psych eval would land him in a seventy-two-hour hold, minimum.

Hallucinations due to grief, a failure to thrive.

He looked up at the branches and greenery clinging to the canopy, defiant trees refusing to die or fall. He laughed before the sound turned into a ragged, heavy sob.

"And on every street corner, you hear," he sang in a whisper.

That's when he heard another crack. He focused his eyes on the enormous tree, the source, he was convinced, of the sound. Eyes strained, he watched, he listened.

It could have been the darkness playing tricks, but Hunter watched the trunk move, the moss fall, taking tree bark with it, like someone was inside, trying to claw their way out.

4

CHAPTER FOUR.

Hunter was too scared to breathe. Dread seeped through him like a frozen river swallowing the earth beneath it. If this were a movie, he would be staring at the screen, yelling for the main character to run, and Sarah would be screaming right along with him. Now he understood them; he was frozen, useless and helpless.

Not ten feet in front of him, the thick old tree wrapped in vines and moss was shedding its skin. There was no one there, no one hacking away at it with a mallet or a hatchet, but bark was flying out violently, hitting him, cutting into the exposed skin of his face.

Still, he didn't move.

His mind screamed.

Get out of here, Hunter. Go now!

Instead, he watched. He watched as something broke through the middle of a tree. It looked like a branch, twisting around in a spiral, a drill burrowing through from the inside of the trunk. A crack, a crevice, formed from above and below that branch, growing deeper, the pitch black of horror and hopelessness seeping out, greeting the forest like an old, ancient friend.

A low rumble, a hum, deep and coarse, seemed to vibrate up from the ground, and the dirt underneath Hunter's feet became death and decay, calling to him, crying to him, singing to him, a song of longing and pain and hurt, a song that promised revenge.

Hunter put his hands over his ears, rocking back and forth on his heels, trying not to absorb any more of the shaking and vibrations, trying to block out the cracking, the sight of a tree splitting in two, unsheathing itself right before him.

"Sarah, I'm so sorry," he sobbed, so terrified that his silence was forcibly broken, as his will bent to the trees, to the haunting that the forest saw fit for him. The spiraling lunged closer, but he kept his eyes shut.

This can't be real.

His mind was surely playing tricks on him.

His eyes squeezed tighter, thinking of Sarah.

The entire town would lock him up if they realized how insane he was becoming. The writhing branch, moving like invisible hands were steering it, was no monster from a children's nightmare. It was just a ghost story to lure tourists to a crumbling old house.

Then why did his heartbeat rise? Why did his inner voice tell him to flee?

There was a tug on his shoe. Something hard wrapped around his ankle. His stomach lurched, bile rising. Hunter's eyes flew open, and a branch was coiling up, moving as if it were alive, there to claim him.

A final crack split the night as the tree broke vertically in half, the moving branch disconnected and now limp. Something new slid out from the bark.

Quiet. It was suddenly so quiet.

Hunter couldn't even hear his own ragged breathing.

There was a foot, bare and petite, that touched the dirt. Then another, a pale leg, hips, a torso forced through the too-tight gap. Hunter stared at skin that nearly glowed, so pale, as if it had never touched the sun.

A ghost.

He had to be hallucinating.

Fingers clutched bark. Skinny arms pushed the rest free. A woman, small, with tangles of dark hair that fell down past her waist. She had eyes that absorbed the colors of the night emerging under heavy lashes. She wore no clothing and made no effort to hide herself. She circled her wrists slowly, eyes locked on Hunter.

Branches were still entangled with his lower half as if they were holding him there for her. He felt like an animal caged in a trap.

Her head tilted. Her pupils dilated. Lips, dark like bruised berries, parted. Her nostrils flared.

Either bile or words would come out of his mouth next.

"H-hello," he choked out. "Do you need help?"

At least it was words.

She was very real. She was flesh, solid, sturdy. It was absurd of him to believe that he was staring at a ghost.

How long have you been out here?

Hunter's fear flipped. A protectiveness suddenly overrode the terror twisting his gut. Whatever she was, whatever nightmare he'd just witnessed, she had to be scared too. The mystery of her coiled around him like smoke, blurring the warning screams in his head. He was entranced, even as his conscience hissed *danger.*

What have you been through?

She lurched forward, limbs awkward at first but gaining power with every step. With her head tucked low, she slammed straight into Hunter's chest. The impact was so fierce from someone so small.

He was on the ground. Blood trickled down his neck after hitting his head on the side of a branch. His vision slightly blurred from the impact. There was a weight on top of him, a body.

Her.

Before he could react, plants and vines coiled around his arms, sprouting from the soil to hold him down and make sure he couldn't run.

"Why did you stop singing?" she asked, her voice low, a savageness in her words, a threat in her question.

Hunter needed to respond. He needed to say something back.

Why aren't you saying anything?

Hunter's mouth opened, but fear strangled every word before it reached his lips. His mind emptied under the weight of her body.

"What were the words? How did the song go?" She slammed her hands on his chest, forcing a wheeze out of him.

"*Dashing through the snow,*" he gasped in tune. "*In a one-horse open sleigh.*"

"I have never heard that song," she said.

"It's a Christmas song." He sucked in air, steadying his breath, though his heart thumped wildly.

She tipped her head back as if listening for a melody in the wind. "I know a Christmas song too, but yours sounds happier than mine."

"Christmas is supposed to be cheerful," he managed. His mind spat curses at him.

What kind of conversation was this?

"Is it really?" Her doubt dripped from each word.

"Why were you in that tree?" He risked the question, but his courage fled when she pressed her chest against his and brushed her nose along his cheek, inhaling him like a wild animal scenting prey.

"You don't smell like the forest," she whispered. She leaped off him so fast he lost track of her for a heartbeat. She moved like no human he'd ever seen.

Her face, though delicate, was older than her fragile body hinted at. He would guess that she was in her early thirties. He heard his father's voice reminding him that women did not like being told how old they looked, so he wisely kept the thought to himself.

"I lost my watch," Hunter blurted, scrambling for sense. "It was a gift. I came back to find it."

She stood above him, legs spread, bending at the waist like a cat about to retch up a nightmare offering. He begged the universe not to let her spit animal bones on him.

"Sweet silver bells," she whispered. Every word dripped like a spell that bound him tighter.

"Is that your Christmas song?"

She flicked her eyes sideways at him, suspicion swirling in her stare.

"How long were you in that tree? Do you need help?" The vines slackened. He rose slowly, extended his hand, and forced calm into his voice. "Come with me. Let me take you home."

"I can never go home." Her words fell softly but seemed to pull the forest into her sadness. "They do not want me back, and the forest will never let me leave."

"But do you want to leave?" he asked, needing to know.

She turned those shadowy eyes on him, blinking as if no one had ever spoken to her that way. "No one has ever asked me that before."

"No one?"

"No one has ever cared what I wanted. Not even the ghosts."

What was he supposed to say to that?

"Do you talk to ghosts often?" He winced at how ridiculous the question sounded.

"They make fine company because they cannot leave you behind. If you want them to stay."

"And you don't want that?"

"Not every soul returns as a ghost. Not everyone finds a reason to linger."

Silence wrapped around them. Her fierceness drooped under the weight of sorrow until her shoulders curled inward. She twirled her hair around her fingers, moonlight trailing her every move but never catching her completely.

"My name is Hunter," he said gently.

"Pleasure," she murmured, then turned away and slipped into the brush.

He stared after her, torn between escaping this nightmare and rescuing her from it. She was real. The forest seemed to bow as she passed, or maybe that was just his fractured mind inventing signs.

What was he going to do, drag her to a police station? Wrap her in blankets? She was fragile yet carved with a grief so deep it made his chest ache.

He hated seeing her pain.

"Wait," he called, trudging after her. His boots squished through mud, so loud and clumsy compared to her quiet, weightless steps. She moved as if she could walk on water.

He struggled to keep her in sight. She did not pause or look back despite his voice breaking the forest hush. Any thought of forcing her anywhere slipped away.

She stopped at the edge of a clearing, and he halted a few paces behind, breathless, soaked through with melting snow.

She turned to him. Her skin shimmered faintly in the moonlight, more ghost than woman in that moment.

"I am sorry," he said, panting. "I just wanted to catch up."

"No one will catch me," she whispered, frowning as if she had just remembered he existed. She raised her hand, and a familiar gleam made his chest tighten.

"This is why you came," she said, examining his watch. "My father owned one like this, but not so flashy."

She had a family.

"Thank you," he murmured, reaching for it. She ignored his hand.

"Who gave it to you? You said it was a gift."

"My wife."

Her eyes widened, shadows deepening the hollows of her cheeks. She stepped back, shaken.

"Forgive me. I did not know you were married."

"What would that change?"

She didn't answer with words. She tossed the watch toward him. He fumbled but caught it and clipped it back on his wrist, relieved.

"I am not married anymore. She passed away."

"Is she buried here in the forest?"

"What? No. Why would she be?"

She stepped closer, her expression softer now. "My father is buried here, among these trees."

"I am sorry to hear that. When did he pass away?"

She looked away. "In 1914."

Hunter let out a laugh he instantly regretted.

"What is funny?" Her voice trembled with an edge of outrage.

"It's just ... it's the year 2025."

"I stopped keeping track of the years a long time ago." She waved her hand, brushing away the passage of time as if it meant nothing. "You should leave now. I do not want to speak with you anymore."

Hunter swallowed a bitter groan. He probably had hit his head harder than he thought.

"I am lost. I do not know how to find my way back. I came from the manor."

"There are many manors here," she said coolly. "Walk that

way, keep the stream behind you, and you will find the one made of red brick." She pointed without looking at him, guiding him away from her and the shattered tree.

"I cannot just leave you here," he said, his voice cracking with guilt and worry. Images of blankets, hospitals, and police officers churned through his mind. "You need help."

"Do I, really?"

She tilted her head slightly, though she still faced away from him.

"Leave now." Her voice grew heavy and powerful, vibrating through the brush until the earth itself seemed to tremble.

You are imagining this. There has to be a rational explanation.

"I am sorry, but I can't just . . ."

She had given him one warning. That was all she would allow. She turned and parted her lips. He thought he heard the first soft notes of a song, but then the world faded until nothing remained except darkness swallowing him whole.

5

CHAPTER FIVE.

Hunter's knuckles throbbed. He had been clutching the worn leather steering wheel for so long that his fingertips had gone numb. In their place was a slow, burning ache, as if the blood had been drained from him. But it wasn't just the blood that was missing.

What am I doing here? How long have I been sitting here?

It took him a moment to unclench each stiff finger. The joints protested with soft cracks. A hiss slipped through his teeth as he forced his fists open, scowling at the dull pain settling in his hands like an old bruise.

You just got off the bus after the field trip. It was the end of the day.

"Hey, you look like shit," Sadie yelled, banging on his window. The sudden noise left Hunter wondering if he was on the verge of a heart attack.

Hunter had been sitting alone in the school parking lot, frost covering most of the glass except for a small patch where his head must have rested, warmed by his breath.

Did I not go home?

He made a mental note not to let anyone know he was losing his memory.

"I'd say call for a sub, but it's the last day before break," Sadie continued. "Throw on a movie and chug a gallon of that crappy coffee from the lounge. You wouldn't get your paid vacation break if you missed the day."

Hunter trembled, pulling his shoulder back to reach for the door handle. A burst of cold air overwhelmed him, the wind whipping the door back so violently that Sadie jumped away before she became a casualty of winter's wrath.

"You look like you haven't gone home, unless your new thing is copying those tech CEOs who wear the same thing every day."

Hunter tried to step out but was yanked back. He clutched his chest while Sadie stared at him like he was a lunatic.

"You gotta take your seatbelt off, chief. You're not drunk, are you? Dear God, please say no."

Hunter shook his head. The click of the buckle released him. The seatbelt slid off his shoulder and retracted behind him.

"Maybe you should take the day off. The principal will freak out, but honestly, those administrators need to be kept on their toes."

"I'm fine, Sadie," Hunter grumbled, standing and shoving the door closed against the wind.

His gold watch jingled with the movement. He stared at it. The last time he was here, he'd been leaving to look for it. Apparently, he had found it. It had gone missing after the field trip. Hadn't it?

"Let's go," he said to Sadie, who was buried in her jacket and faux fur hood, her glasses fogging with every breath. "I'll need all the coffee I can get."

They trudged across the icy parking lot. Cars with music blaring cut too close to buses as they skidded around corners.

No matter how many warning letters the PTO sent out, there was always a nanny or older sibling driving like the staff were expendable obstacles.

"That's Connor's dad's new fling," Sadie huffed. "Met her last week at the conference. She bragged that her sugar daddy bought her that dark blue Mercedes with all the extras. He made sure the seats go all the way back."

Hunter nearly choked on laughter but masked it as a cough. When he recovered, he smirked at her.

"There's my guy," she said, winking as Hunter held the door for her. Their wet boots made new puddles for the janitor to mop once the bell rang. The taupe linoleum floors and dark blue lockers all reeked of bleach. Someone must have thrown up here after school yesterday.

They sauntered down the hall and into the mustard-colored teacher's lounge. It was buzzing, staff laughing around a big table of small gifts glinting under harsh fluorescent lights.

Sadie shrugged off her coat and stuffed it in her cubby next to his. Hunter did the same, doing his best to look normal.

You are fine. Nothing has happened to you.

But he couldn't shake the feeling that something had. He'd woken up in his car as if he'd never left, watch back on his wrist.

He tried to push it down as Sadie grabbed an oddly shaped gift wrapped in red paper with gold polka dots.

"Shit," he muttered.

Sadie's face fell. "Are you kidding me? You forgot? It's going to ruin the game."

Hunter hadn't forgotten the teacher gift exchange. It was sitting at home on his desk, wrapped and ready.

"I'll run and grab it at lunch. It's at home."

"You better. This is the only day all year I hang around this place when I don't have to, and you know it."

Hunter did know it. He looked around the lounge: five

small circular tables, a counter with a sink, and the fresh smell of brewing coffee drifting over him. The warmth grounded him. He let his shoulders drop as Darius Reed, the special projects teacher, strolled over and held up a hand for a high-five, then pulled Hunter in for a hug.

"You have no idea how relieved I am that you're taking my kids part of today," Hunter said. His students spent ninety minutes each week in art and then went to Darius for science and STEM projects.

"Rough night?" Darius asked.

"I couldn't tell you," Hunter laughed.

"Damn, man. I know it's the holidays, but maybe save the eggnog until after today."

"Good advice," Hunter said.

"I knew it!" Sadie shouted over her shoulder, dropping her gift on the table.

"Don't listen to her. She's nuts," Hunter said.

"We're all a little nuts," Darius said before launching into a passionate explanation about the compost worms they'd be using today.

Celia and Elaine were sipping coffee in the corner. Celia, one of the sixth-grade teachers, wore bold eyeliner. Her chin-length platinum hair bounced perfectly even on the rainiest days. Elaine, the music teacher, had sharp gray eyes and dark auburn hair. She was the one who forced every class to participate in the dreaded holiday pageant.

Hunter had just survived that last weekend.

"I'm so tired of big dick energy," Celia said.

"I'm with you. Let's make it big vagina energy. The patriarchy doesn't get to say smaller is better," Elaine replied.

"I love this. The bigger the vagina, the more tongues I can fit inside," Celia said.

"Now that should be the goal," Elaine agreed.

"Ladies, you're on school property," Principal Keanin

muttered as he passed, coffee in hand, escaping before they could respond.

Hunter kept his eyes firmly on the floor, but it didn't save him.

"We need to get you a . . . less sad . . . hobby, Hunter," Elaine said dryly. "The poor widower vibe is getting old."

"I like it. It's gothic, dramatic," Celia added, sipping her coffee.

"Suggestions?" Hunter asked. Elaine raised an eyebrow.

"Get certified in piercings. Side hustle. Bad economy."

"Is it a hobby if it makes money?"

"Yes," Elaine said as Celia said, "No."

Hunter sighed and grabbed his favorite mug, round and speckled blue. It was a gift from one of his first students back when he still had hope this job wouldn't eat him alive.

The hot, steaming liquid bounced in and around the interior until it found its smooth collective rhythm. Hunter followed the pour with two organic brown sugar packets and stirred, looking out at the rest of the staff that was trudging in and out of the lounge. The warmth and promise of a few weeks of rest put most of their faces at ease.

"Hunter, I know you're coming to the Christmas market with us!" Nina, the bubbly kindergarten teacher, squealed as she tossed her gift on the table. She winked at him before heading for Malcolm, the stoic kindergarten teacher.

"I'll be there," he said, lifting his cup in salute.

The first bell rang. Everyone sighed and shuffled into the hall toward their classrooms.

As the caffeine hit his empty stomach, Hunter's hands grew clammy. He stepped into Room Eleven. Papers flew through the air, phones flashed, and half his students were eating holiday cookies before lunch.

"Now, now," Hunter called, quieting the room. "You might

think I'd let you slack off today, but state tests are in four months. Might be smart to start early."

The room froze.

"I'm kidding." He grinned and set his coffee down. "Now, who's got cookies? I need one."

The morning blurred past. When the lunch bell rang, Hunter checked for his keys, heard them jingle, and followed his class out. He didn't have much time, but if he didn't get that gift, Sadie would hound him for eternity.

Snow mounded along the streets as he steered home. He parked, crunching through his unshoveled driveway, promising himself he'd salt it tonight. The last shriveled leaf clung to the tree over his roof.

Inside, the wooden floors creaked beneath him. A fireplace sat under a stone facade. Tiny painted yellow flowers dotted the white walls—Sarah's half-finished project.

People told him to get a hobby. Sarah had had a million. After she died, Hunter spent years finishing her projects, like painting those hundreds of flowers.

They'd bought this place together. He couldn't really afford it now; the accident payout helped with the mortgage, but it would run out soon. He'd have to sell eventually.

No couch, just a massive desk covered in paint stains and marker scars. His teacher's gift sat on top, wrapped in green paper and way too much tape.

His stomach growled. He stepped into the kitchen, where the fridge still smelled like vinegar and brine from Sarah's pickling obsession. He kept the jars out of guilt. Now he pickled onions and tomatoes himself. He regretted trying it with eggs.

Hunter grabbed a yogurt hidden behind the jars, flipped on his old radio, and holiday music filled the kitchen. Peeling back the lid, he licked the sweet pink yogurt and moaned at the sugar hit.

"Jingle bells, jingle bells, jingle all the way," he sang, wiggling his hips as he spooned more yogurt.

A flash of movement in the dark, a tree falling apart, etched its way into his mind, and Hunter stopped moving. His yogurt was now on the floor, the clang of his spoon bouncing twice before it rested on the cheap linoleum tile.

Her.

He knew now. He hadn't come home because he'd met her.

He stared out the back window at the snow-covered yard.

Was it real?

It felt real.

If it was, he'd left her out there.

Is she still alive?

His fingers hovered over 911. But what if he was losing it? If it were real, doing nothing was worse than being embarrassed.

He dialed.

"Sadie, it's Hunter. Emergency. Cover for me."

He didn't wait for her reply before he hung up. Hunter bolted to his car. His phone buzzed. Sadie's calls and texts exploded onto his screen.

SADIE 5:23 AM:

You better not be dying or I'm calling your mom.

"Fuck," he hissed, slamming the wheel.

HUNTER 5:23 AM:

Will explain later. Please cover my class.

He skidded into the estate parking lot. Maybe the security cameras would flag him for showing up so often. He didn't care. He sprinted, lungs burning, boots thudding in fresh snow.

"I'm coming," he gasped.

You should really start jogging.

He ran past the brick mansion, deeper onto the grounds. He pictured her lying there, blue lips, empty eyes, finding her too late.

Sarah would never forgive him for that. He wouldn't forgive himself either.

His watch clinked with each step. His boots left a clear trail in the untouched snow.

You didn't imagine it. You're not crazy.

But maybe it would be easier if he were. Then she'd be safe. There'd be no danger.

He pushed into the trees. The snow stopped crunching, replaced by ice crackling under the canopy. Light barely cut through.

"Hello?" His voice cracked. He cleared his throat, stepping over bushes and dead leaves. Birds and squirrels scattered. He fought to keep his heartbeat steady.

"Ma'am, are you there?" Louder now, more certain.

I'll find you. I'm here.

The memory sharpened: a body stepping from inside a tree. Skin like moonlight. He swallowed, terrified of what he'd do if he actually found her.

You were here. You talked to her.

Hunter leaned against a tree, breath clouding in the cold.

Please don't let this be in my head.

He crossed a stream, calling out. He searched for a sign, a hand, a foot—anything in the snow.

Nothing here. No one here.

Minutes passed. Panic bled into dread, then doubt.

Hunter bent, catching his breath.

What is wrong with you?

His shoulders shook. He sobbed alone. His cries leaked out all the grief he'd bottled up, freezing on his cheeks.

You'll get fired.

Good.

Something had to change. He couldn't fake normal anymore. He needed to break before he broke something worse.

His cries died. The forest kept his secrets.

Get up. Get out. Grab the gift.

Might as well face everyone one last time. The students who weirdly liked him. The coworkers who pretended not to notice he was unraveling.

He stood, coughing in the cold, wiping spit and tears away. He pulled out his phone and turned toward the old mansion, toward the garden where he'd married Sarah.

"Oh, what fun," he whispered to calm himself as he trudged back through the dark.

"It is to ride in a one-horse open sleigh—"

He stopped. A tree cracked apart in the shadows.

"Why did you stop singing?" a woman's voice asked.

I'm not crazy.

6

CHAPTER SIX.

"It's you," Hunter said, staring into the darkness, staring at the figure before him that had escaped his memory yet haunted his day, like a siren at sea, calling him back to her. "You're real. You're actually real and . . . I found you."

"Hmmm." She seemed disappointed.

"I . . . I came back. I think I came back for you," he breathed.

"You shouldn't have."

Hunter was at a loss. He didn't know what to say or do.

He hadn't expected to find her.

But she didn't need saving.

How do I help you?

"What do you remember?" she asked him. "From meeting me."

Maybe I'm the one who needs saving.

"You should come back with me." Hunter ignored her question. The answer was *nothing*.

He watched the woman turn her head away. Her dark hair was long, draped over her nude body like a fur cloak. Her skin was tinged with purples and blues. He could see the goosebumps that covered her, the cuts, small crevices of deep red that were not yet scabbed over, proof enough that she was real, existing outside of his imagination.

She was so small, so frail, that Hunter knew that he needed to get her fed, clothed, and warm.

"I can save you," he whispered, holding onto the belief he'd come there with.

But you couldn't save Sarah.

"Let me save you." He held out his hand to her. She turned and looked down at it, his outstretched palm, fingers reaching, pleading. "I can't just leave you here."

She cocked her head, face blank at first, but then she flashed a smile.

"I haven't left this forest in over one hundred years."

That was a delusion, wasn't it? It had to be.

Something in his gut, though, told him it was not. He chose to ignore it; he had to.

What do you say now?

"Why did you come here in the first place?" The conversation was good. She wasn't accepting his hand, but she wasn't running.

"A boy." She sneered at him, like he was the boy, like he had done this to her. Hunter took a step back. He wasn't sure why, but for the first time, he got the sense that she was more than a lost soul in the woods. This woman was perhaps not a woman; perhaps a monster hid under that skin-cloak. An eerie prickle climbed up the back of his neck; the silence around them was too profound, as if they were in a vacuum, where no one could walk up to them, and no one could find them.

"A boy called me a witch in front of my family, at our Christmas ball. I ran, I ran, and I sang, and the greenery rose up to defend me. People screamed, some cried, and if I ever saw that boy again, I would kill him in an instant."

Hunter was stunned.

Say anything.

"If this happened in 1914, then that boy is already dead now."

Good. That seemed good.

She studied his face, unmoving, standing with her legs wide, her arms wrapped around her waist. The severity in her eyes softened.

"How dreary," she said. "Disappointing, really. I only leave my tree looking for him, singing at the edge of the forest, trying to lure him back to me. But then I heard you sing . . ."

"Does that mean that you'll come with me then?" Hunter asked. "Or will you go back to your tree forever?"

She was crazy, delusional, just like he thought he was.

You're just as crazy as her, but at least you have clothes on.

She didn't answer. She just stared, her gaze unapologetic, unfaltering. Hunter wondered if she would run, like a frightened squirrel, if he moved, if he made a sound. There was no fear there, though. The way that she looked at him was the way a predator lazily let its prey walk by because it had already eaten that day.

"Every time I leave my tree, my body ages," she whispered after some time. "My breasts are larger, my hips are more spread. I have urges."

Hunter's eyes immediately fell to his feet, his stomach jumping.

"What?"

He was confused. Why would she say that here?

"How old were you when you came into the forest?" he asked.

"Fourteen."

"How old are you now?"

"One hundred and fourteen, maybe older. The urges—they became unbearable only a few years after I sealed myself in the tree."

"So these urges ... you've never been touched?" He cleared his throat.

Why the fuck are you talking about this?

"Touched?" she asked, her words slithering, snake-like, like he was being lured into a trap.

"I touch myself all the time. I make the branches grow and massage the walls inside of me until I scream and pant until I have no voice left. Then it's time to go back into my tree."

Hunter's eyes widened, his jaw dropped.

You're not hearing her right.

One thing he knew, though, was that she wasn't coming with him. She wouldn't let him help her, save her. He'd found no damsel. There was no distress.

"Do you want to see?" she asked, no smile on her face, a seriousness with no humor, no sarcasm. Hunter's mouth dropped.

"Do I want to see what?"

The woman smiled as she opened her mouth, a song escaping, ethereal notes pouring out. The forest reacted instantly, the trees and bushes around Hunter growing and shifting until a branch grew out to her, smooth with a medium thickness.

"I would sit on this," she said, breaking it off. "And writhe around until I am filled with stars, it's the only other time I can see them since I stay under the cover of the trees."

She moved the branch down her breast, circling it down her navel. Hunter let his eyes linger. His stomach tightened as her hand, her tool, came down to her pelvis, gliding to her upper thigh as she pushed in, ripping her skin.

"No," he had to yell. Panic overtook him.

"Why?" she asked him.

"It's not right." He knew how annoying that sounded. He was irritated with himself that it was the only thing he could think to say. It was how he felt, though.

I can't stand here and watch. I can't take advantage.

"I came here to help you," he said. "But you don't want help."

She was silent, her eyes large and sparkling with what he thought was anger and rejection. If what she said was true, then she likely didn't get told no too often.

You offended her, you idiot.

The bulge in his pants was offended, too.

"I can go," he said, not knowing now what to do. It seemed the safest thing. She wasn't frostbitten, she wasn't crying, she wasn't asking for help. Hunter knew when to leave; he knew when he wasn't welcome.

You're going to lose your job over this.

The light, cheery singing of birds skipping through the treetops helped him refocus, recenter, bringing his heart and breath back to a normal rhythm.

"It was nice to meet you," he said, turning in the direction of the mansion and estate. He took a few steps, the sounds of the forest crackling and whooshing around him from his movement, from the life and energy he had sacrificed to the trees. It felt like little pieces of his soul as he prepared to go back to his car, now knowing he was perfectly sane, but still leaving a woman alone in the forest, so vulnerable, so unprotected.

I'm sorry, Sarah. I did try.

He was sorry for many reasons. Too many to count.

"Olivia."

Hunter stopped mid-step, his foot hovering. He took her in again; her chin was raised high, and the anger ebbed from her gaze. She wasn't smiling. She wasn't friendly.

"What was that?"

She took in a breath, her dark hair framing her sharp features. "You asked my name. It is Olivia."

A tear ran down her cheek.

"Why are you crying?"

She shook her head.

"I understand," he said. "I cry, too."

"My father, he was the last one to say my name out loud."

Over one hundred years ago.

It's not real, Hunter.

Hunter began stepping back toward her as the strength she presented slowly melted away. He put his hand up to her cheek. She flinched, but let him touch her, lips parted, nearly trembling.

Hunter looked into her dark eyes.

Beautiful. She was devastatingly beautiful.

"Olivia," he said. "It's nice to meet you."

"Will you come back?" she asked.

Hunter forgot to breathe. It was the way she looked at him, the way her haunting gaze bore into his soul, as if she saw something there, something he didn't know about, lying dormant, waiting to impress her. There was an expectation.

What do you need?

"Do you want me to come back?" Hunter asked.

"Hmmm."

Her interest seemed fading; whatever she hoped to pull out of him wasn't coming forward. Her eyes went vacant, her long lashes brushing her cheeks again while she blinked, unmoving, unshifting, still as an ancient tree.

It suddenly felt so wrong now to walk away. He was planted, rooted there with her. He could stay within her energy all day, even though he wasn't sure how to handle it, how to act right around her.

Olivia.

Her name wrapped around his mind, a song stuck in his head, one that would never leave him.

"Please," he whispered one last time. "Come with me."

Olivia smiled, and as she opened her mouth, a song came out. Hunter only heard the first few words, a magic filling him like a parasite, a love bomb that soothed him into a blank state.

"Hark how the bells,
Sweet silver bells
All seems to say
Throw cares away."

Hunter blacked out, though he stood firm. His eyes rolled to the back of his head, his fists clenched at his sides. His body responded to her song, to magic that made him move closer to the enchanting voice that brought his body into hers.

Hunter's mouth opened as he completed her song in a stunned mental paralysis.

"Christmas is here, bringing good cheer."

Olivia let her tongue slide over her front teeth before smiling at him, her new pet, her spellbound doll, a soon-to-be lover where neither would ever relent. The forest obeyed her song, her will as well, as it grew up and around him, binding him. She walked forward, her bare feet in the cold, in the dirt, unbothered. She was safe there with him. She leaned forward, her lips about to touch the pale, flushed flesh of his cheek, her breasts pressing up against him.

She didn't kiss him, though; this wasn't their moment.

As she walked away, the forest let him go too, his feet taking him out of the trees, back to the parking lot, where he would once again wake up in the car, forgetting what had happened.

7

CHAPTER SEVEN.

SADIE 7:35 P.M.

You won the stupid raffle. Everyone's pissed.

SADIE 7:39 P.M.

Dude, are you okay?

SADIE 7:42 P.M.

You've been acting really off lately.

SADIE 8:02 P.M.

Raffle prize is two tickets to the holiday ball.
No, I don't want to be your date.

SADIE 9:04 P.M.

They're considering redrawing since you're not
here.

SADIE 9:09 P.M.

Never mind, you won. No one else wants the
prize.

SADIE 9:14 P.M.

I guess I'd go, and we could make fun of
everyone. But only if I can bring my cat.

SADIE 10:00 P.M.

Don't mind me, just sloshed in the teacher's
lounge.

SADIE 10:01 P.M.

I don't think you'll be fired as long as you have
a good fucking excuse. You're welcome.

Hunter sniffed. He felt like shit, grabbing the bridge of his nose just above his eyes as his head throbbed. With blurred vision that only cleared after a few blinks, he stared at the phone in his hand.

2:00 a.m.

The steering wheel in front of him confirmed that he was in his car. His watch, Sarah's watch, gleamed on his wrist, the blue light illuminating the fine metal. It was cold, windows frosted over with no light outside.

This felt familiar, though. He couldn't quite tell how or why, but what Hunter did know was that he had no clue, no indication of why he was there, and that gave him that inescapable, suffocating feeling of déjà vu.

Sarah, what is wrong with me?

Hunter turned the key in the ignition, sitting there with a headache as he waited for his windows to defrost. Once they did, the square campus of his elementary school came into focus. Even the streetlights were turned off at this hour.

Hunter picked up his phone and texted Sadie back.

HUNTER 2:01 AM

> I've been throwing up all night. Thanks for covering.

This is who he was now, lying about being sick, waking up with no idea of why he was sitting in his car in the middle of the night. It felt like he had been under a spell, a haze encompassing him, a lullaby, a voice that he could almost hear, singing to him, clinging to him, refusing to let go.

There is no song.

Hunter turned his head to the passenger seat, imagining the infectious smile Sarah gave him after she'd playfully hit him in the shoulder. He would have been making fun of her, maybe for whatever her newest hobby was. That food scientist's paycheck had to go somewhere, and they could only travel in the summer because of Hunter's school schedule.

Mushroom foraging it is.

Hunter liked to imagine still living in the bubble of love he had once thrived in. One that maybe he hadn't deserved.

Go home. Just drive home.

The last thing he needed was to get pulled over by security and alert the school that he was lurking in the parking lot after calling out sick during school hours. Hunter put his foot on the gas and began the short drive home. If he wanted to stare out the window in the darkness, he could at least be parked in his own driveway.

Whatever was going on with him, he needed to figure it out fast. He knew he'd left the school in a panic. He remembered something, something so important that it had been worth putting the one thing he had on the line: his career. Not that he was a career kind of guy, but he also didn't normally rock the boat. He didn't mind safe. He didn't mind stable.

That's why he had fallen in love with Sarah, because she was the opposite, filled with light and a healthy amount of chaos.

Why did you leave? Where were you going?

Hunter had half an urge to call his mom and inquire about their family's mental health history. A call this late would surely cause problems for him, though. He didn't need his parents to worry, to drop their overly comfortable retirements and dote on him.

You know that they would love to.

They liked having something to do, someone to focus on. Especially his mom.

The car was parked. Hunter blinked back in disbelief that he wasn't home. Time seemed to have skipped. He was so wrapped up in his head that his body took over, and a ten-minute drive turned into something longer.

He was in another parking lot, not the school's, and certainly not his driveway. A large, towering estate stood eerily in the dark. He was back at their wedding venue, the trees swaying in the distance, a dark, ominous dance, twisting and bowing to the snow flurries drifting through the night air.

Vultauge Manor.

That lullaby, that haze that clouded him, urged him to step out of the car as he squinted in the dark, trying to see some-thing, anything. He heard a voice, one so beautiful, so heart-breaking that it felt like the world was crying, melting, then freezing back solid while encompassing Hunter's body within it.

Sarah.

No, it wasn't Sarah. It was a spirit of a different nature. Where Sarah had been filled with light, this one was filled with darkness, the kind that existed only in the deepest depths of the ocean, hiding secrets while life floated by at the surface.

Hunter saw a wisp of her breath, a ghost floating up over her head, but proof that she was there, proof that she was not a spirit, a hallucination.

So familiar. Even this, even her.

He walked right toward her, though he carried trepidation in his heart. His head told him something different; it told him he needed to get to the bottom of this, to figure out what was wrong with him, so he could decide if it was worth fixing.

The distance between them closed as his strides grew long and quick, stars peeking out from behind the clouds of the night sky, which moved quickly, pushed by the wind that plagued the grounds and slapped his cheeks in an unwelcoming way.

"You came back," that voice, that song that followed him, infected his heart.

It's you.

Hunter shook his head as if trying to clear a blockage in his ears, in his mind. Something was there, something was in the way, and he knew he knew the nude woman whose feet stood in snow at the edge of the Berkshires, dark hair wrapping around her body.

"I came back," he replied.

She stared at him, her smile mischievous, even conniving, as if he had walked right into her plan, her trap.

Maybe he did.

"You shouldn't be able to remember. Not this soon."

"It looks like I do," he lied.

"When I sing, you forget. You come to me or obey my heart's song, as does the forest, as do the plants."

Hunter cocked his head.

"A siren," he said.

"I don't know that word," she admitted after a beat of silence.

"A witch," he clarified. "Who lives in the water, singing to sailors."

Her smile and the ease of her posture disappeared as her eyes narrowed, the energy around them threatening.

"I am not a witch," she said, enunciating every word clearly, quietly. He had struck a nerve. It was too obvious with the darkening of her eyes, the start of a snarl on her upper lip.

Dangerous. She's dangerous. She's real.

She stepped forward, moving fast, a panther jumping on its prey. Hunter flinched, leaning away, but she didn't let him. Instead, her hands found both sides of his neck, pulling him down towards her.

Her lips pressed into his. Hunter could have collapsed into her, his body so tense, so unsure.

Trust, it seemed to be telling him, urging him. The contact seemed to break the spell that he was under, the haze lifting as his memory came flooding back. It crashed down hard, and his heart ached. His body hardened while he opened his mouth to let her tongue find his. The first time someone else's lips had touched his since Sarah.

She caressed him, both with her hands and with her tongue, as her touch fell from his neck and moved down to his shoulders. Hunter kissed her back, but his hands were awkwardly by his sides. She fixed that as hers slid down his arms, fingers intertwining. His hands were so large and dominating over hers. Despite how powerful he thought she must be, Olivia fit into him so well. It was like she was made for him, and he was made for her.

He pulled away, gasping for breath.

"Olivia," he said, memories trickling back in.

She smiled, not a hint of viciousness. Hunter wished he could interpret that smile, decide if there was sadness or true happiness behind it. It was neither, but something that existed in between. An utter mystery in the battered, powerful goddess he stood before. A woman who was so goddamn terrifying, but also endearing.

She was in his arms. Her skin wasn't soft, but she smelled of earth mixed with root beer, like the inner bark of a sassafras tree. It put him at ease, her scent, and he had to remind himself not to close his eyes and fall into her hair, the cold tying them together, a blanket of fate.

What her mind must be thinking, feeling, with him on her breath was something he was dying to know. One hundred years in this forest without companionship had to make her challenging.

"I call you Hunter, then?" she asked, the hint of a threat, the hint of the gaze he'd seen when he had uttered the word *witch*, swirled to the surface of those eyes, the color of a deep abyss, the dirt found at the bottom of ancient volcanoes.

It was easy to look past that threat this time, upon hearing his name on her lips. He nearly lost his breath, as if he had been sprinting here to get to her, sprinting to the forest only to listen to her voice do him the service of acknowledging him.

You can't leave her here.

Hunter opened a hand to her, and she stared at it, confusion evident in her furrowed brow.

"It's my hand," he said. "Please take it, and I'll guide you to my home."

She sighed, another strike against him evident in the sudden slouch of her shoulders, the skin around her belly button pinching together, creating a cute pouch that accentuated her womanly figure. A figure he couldn't ignore a feral attraction toward, one that had him walking on eggshells as he spoke to her, as he looked at her. It was the first time he had truly wanted someone, needed someone, since Sarah.

Sarah.

An overwhelming, heart-aching sadness hit Hunter, an arrow piercing him clean through.

"Sing that song," Olivia said.

"What?" Hunter wasn't there anymore; the fantasy had broken. The spell was overshadowed by the betrayal that now felt very real to him, his betrayal of Sarah.

That kiss.

"I will go with you," Olivia clarified. "If you sing that song. I've never heard anything like that. It was so, so . . . "

"Cheery," Hunter suggested.

Olivia just stared at him.

Cutting her off, another strike perhaps.

Despite the waves of emotions, the concussion, the arousal, the relief, the despair, Hunter wanted so badly to save her, to bring Olivia out from the forest. He took a deep inhale, and on his exhale, his voice boomed, so deep, vibrating down through the roots of the greenery he stood within.

Hunter cleared his throat, finding his voice, the voice he had lost when he lost Sarah, the voice inside him that once laughed and meant it, that nurtured students with a passion, that loved, that loved so hard it molded him.

Maybe it was finally time to have a voice like that again.

Sarah, did you send her?

It was a leap, but he had nothing else to go on. There was no other way to justify bringing along a deranged stranger, drawn in by the childlike holiday songs he hummed.

"Jingle bells,

Jingle bells,

Jingle all the way."

Olivia's face lit up, awe and wonder speckled her cheeks like glitter falling from the trees above her. She opened her mouth, filling herself with music, and began her duet.

"Sweet silver bells, all things to say, throw cares away."

Hunter felt the power; he felt the forest shift, creaking and growing while his vision faded in and out. She stopped when she noticed him stumble, despite standing still, towering over her.

"I'll come," she whispered, putting her hand in his.

Hunter stared at that hand, at her skin so pale it looked bathed in moonlight, even though it couldn't shine through the thick clouds of forest trees.

"Your heart," Olivia said, her eyes moving up to catch his, to keep him in her spell. "It's beating so loud. Is that for me?"

For her.

It was because Hunter felt terror trying to overshadow his chivalry, his bravery. This woman would change his life, and he feared he might regret it, regret helping someone who wasn't asking for help.

But maybe she can help you.

Hunter found a speck of courage. He only needed a little to convince himself that this was right. That he would do this for anyone, not just a beautiful woman who kissed him, who pulled him so far into her that he may soon struggle for air, drowning in those enchanting eyes.

"Yes," he answered. "My heart is beating for you."

With that, Olivia took her first step out from under the trees since she had fled there, looking for shelter, looking for safety, looking for the acceptance of the plants and the trees. Here was the first person she might be able to trust since her father had died.

Olivia's grip was crushing, tight, as if she might never again let go of Hunter's hand.

He didn't mind.

8

CHAPTER EIGHT.

"I hear these," Olivia said, staring in wonder at the beige-gray faux leather dashboard of Hunter's parked car. Her eyes were wide, curious, but still sharp, ready to bolt at the slightest threat.

"They have the strangest hum that I could never place before."

She was some kind of siren; it was the closest story he could relate to her from his childhood. There was no ocean, no sailors being lured to their deaths. Instead, it was him, maybe others too, being drawn to her, but also forgetting. Where memories should be, there was only haze, a cloud that swirled inside him.

He hoped he had broken it, this spell. That whatever it was, now that he knew of it, it would no longer affect him.

That's a stupid thing to think. You are far from being safe.

"When I step towards the edge of the forest, I can hear these carriages from the roads in the distance, in the quiet of the night. They sound like monsters with strange music, with that hum."

Hunter followed her gaze, then flicked his eyes down to her

bare shoulders. A shiver ran through her, and her arms crossed tight over her breasts. Without thinking, he shrugged off his own coat and draped it around her shoulders, limbs awkward in their intimate space.

"Here," he murmured. "You're freezing."

She flinched at first, then tugged the coat closer, burying her hands in the sleeves.

Hunter turned the key in the ignition. The vibration of the seats and the roar of the engine sent a thrill up his spine as he watched Olivia squeal and throw her hands over her ears. Hunter got that same thrill from rollercoasters that he had no business riding at this age.

Of course, he didn't have Sarah to drag him on them anymore.

"You're actually here," Hunter breathed, disbelief starting to sink in.

"Yes," she replied as if it were a perfectly normal question.

"You really have never been in a car before."

"No. My father would ride in one going into the city. It looked nothing like this."

"You've never spoken on a phone before."

"A phone?"

Hunter pulled his out to show her. She squinted at the blue light in the dark.

"You're really from 1914."

"I am."

Hunter put his foot on the gas, and Olivia gasped at the forward trajectory, headlights guiding the way.

"Why me? Why did you choose to trust me?"

Olivia was quiet for a moment, collecting her answer. "The plants, the forest, the earth, it pulses, it makes music for me, to tell me I'm safe, to tell me I belong. You're the first person who has ever sung back to me. So perhaps, it told me that with you, I could belong too."

Hunter's stomach dropped at the no-nonsense declaration of hope and love. He didn't know if he was ready for that, ready for anything more than just knowing that she was out of the forest, out of the trees, that she was safe and thriving.

"I might still take you to the police station," he blurted out.

Idiot.

"You could still be a missing person. You could be injured, and you could not know what's happened to you," he tried to reason, mostly with himself.

How can I accept with no question what she's telling me? What if I make the situation worse?

His memory was fuzzy. Was there something else that had happened? Something he couldn't remember?

Olivia laughed, a full, outright, guttural laugh that felt like she was spitting out butterflies and woodland faerie creatures. It was a delight, infectious. Hunter couldn't help but grin like a madman. He could live there, in that laugh, forever.

That's a crazy thought to have. You are acting crazy.

Rational, he could be rational.

"Right, the police station it is."

But even as he said it, he knew he wouldn't.

She wasn't from 1914. It was impossible. Some sort of physics law would have to be broken. She had lost her memory, her mind.

So have you.

They drove in silence, and whenever Hunter pulled his eyes off the road, allowing himself seconds of peering at Olivia, the very real woman who sat near naked in his passenger seat, he smiled. She was enraptured with the world outside her window, looking at every streetlight, every building that they passed with complete wonderment. With the heater on, color flushed back into her milky-white skin, a porcelain doll that had been lost in the woods, now with a glow, a vibrant pink hue on her lips, her cheeks, and down her neck.

Hunter forced his gaze back onto the road, but it was so hard to look away, so hard not to be enraptured with her. Any control he had was slipping. He would soon be putty under that terrifying gaze that she had—that gaze could control him. Perhaps already had.

No, that's crazy. There's no such thing as sirens.

"What will happen to me?" Her words were soft, hesitant. She looked at him, her chin turning over her shoulder while she kept her body wound together, her legs tucked into her chest, the seatbelt pushing against her hips, creating cute ripples and pinches in her skin. "The police will lock me up. I will be in a cage as they poke me, laugh at me. Look at the witch."

Hunter blinked, not expecting such sad words when her face was still in awe, as she still pointed and whispered to herself when they drove by a Christmas tree farm.

"They call them cells now. Did they use cages back then? Why would they lock you up? They will help you."

"How? How would they help me?"

Hunter turned left, driving further into town.

"Maybe they could find your family. Find someone that you know."

"I am over one hundred years old. I don't have any family. I've murdered my own father. I am not a child. They will put me on the street. Then, I walk back to my trees, back to my forest."

Fair.

Rational decisions were for the weak anyway.

Hunter flipped the car around in a U-turn, the wheels skidding on some ice on the road. Olivia let out a squeal, one that seemed equal parts thrilled and surprised, judging by the way her hands gripped the ceiling of the car, by the way her face lit up, her teeth dazzled behind her lips. Hunter's erratic driving, his discovery of Olivia's hidden need for thrill-seeking so close to the police station in the dark hours of the morning, attracted a flash of lights, blue and red, in his rearview mirror.

Of course. I guess the police will find us.

Hunter could imagine the texts from Sadie now.

> What did you do on the first day of winter break?

> I spent it in a jail cell because I was driving like a psychopath with a nude, battered woman in my driver's seat.

Getting out of this seemed pretty unlikely.

"I have to pull over. That is the police." Hunter said.

"You're upset," she said.

"This isn't good," he said, putting his foot on the brake, his tire hitting the curb on the sidewalk.

"I can kill him," she offered as the policeman got out of his vehicle, the sound of his boots crunching on ice and slush.

"Please don't," Hunter said, reaching over Olivia, who watched his hand like it was a snake that could bite her. He opened the glove compartment, taking out his registration.

"Why not?" Olivia was undoubtedly offended that he didn't take her up on her generous offer, crossing her arms in front of her chest, her bottom lip pouting.

He paid too much attention to that bottom lip, remembering what it felt like against his.

Knock. Knock. Knock.

The sound of knuckles against his window pulled Hunter out of his trance, his eyes pulled away from her pouting, juicy lip, and toward the cop on the other side of his window, shining a flashlight down at him.

"Because it's too close to Christmas," Hunter answered Olivia, and he rolled his window down.

That's the best you could come up with?

"Son, do you know why I pulled you over?" the cop asked, shivering in the snow, his head bobbing a little.

He shone his flashlight at Olivia, who cowered away from the attention.

"Would you believe me if I told you I was heading to the police station?" Hunter asked nervously. He was no outlaw. He didn't do bad things; he was a goddamn elementary school teacher, and this . . . this looked very bad.

"I'm going to need you to step out of the car, sir," the officer said. "Ma'am, are you alright?"

Hunter obeyed, the click of his seatbelt loud in the quiet. The cop's badge read Mason. Hunter knew that name. He'd taught so many Mason kids over the years.

"Hunter, let's go," Olivia called softly. He looked back. She had one knee hiked onto the dashboard, showing them everything.

"Take me home now."

"I have to make sure you're not in danger, ma'am," Mason stammered, mouth hanging open. "I see bruises and cuts under that jacket. Where did you get those?"

"Do you ask your wife the same questions when you're staring at another woman?" Olivia giggled.

Mason recoiled, face flushing red.

"I'll be taking you both back to the station. There are clothes there to get her covered up," he said, hand on his radio mic.

Olivia lunged forward, crawling across the seats, her face going void, empty. Then she changed, alive with rapture as her mouth opened. Her voice poured out, a hum that tangled around Hunter's mind. A lullaby, a death promise, a black hole.

This didn't happen last time.

Jump in.

Her song lured him toward that darkness. Hunter stepped

forward, eyes locked on the void, blind to the car, the cop, the world.

Vines, black and purple, unfurled around him. Thorns pulsed at their tips, begging him closer. He wanted to touch them. He wanted to feel the prick on his skin.

Metal clanked against his watch. Hunter's hand hit the car frame and snapped him out of it. His vision cleared. The police car engine roared, tires squealed. Snow and slush sprayed up his legs as Mason fled, disappearing into the night.

Hunter turned to Olivia. She sat back in the passenger seat, calm as a queen.

"What do you see?" Her song was gone. Her scent, earth and rain still overwhelmed him.

Why am I standing here?

"I've never seen it before, someone resisting my song. What did you see?"

I resisted her song?

A crash cracked the night—glass, metal, a sickening pop. Hunter ducked behind the door. Down the street, the patrol car had plowed through a general store's front window. Mason's body lay half on the hood, half inside, unmoving, a dark pool spreading under his hand.

"What did you do?" Hunter's voice shook, small and stunned. His brave self, his rational mind, was gone. "We should call someone. He needs help."

He noticed that there were no other witnesses. It was just them and the midnight silence interrupted by the shrieking alarm.

Your phone. Get your phone.

He crawled into the driver's seat, slammed the door.

"Finally." Olivia clapped her hands. "It's new, you know, not getting my way. I was a child running from a ball. Since then, no one says no to me."

"I didn't say no," Hunter said, the glow of his phone blue on his face.

Sirens wailed in the distance. Help was coming. Too late for Mason. Too late for Hunter's old life.

Get her out of here.

If he'd stayed away, convinced himself she wasn't real, Mason would still be alive.

Guilt slithered through him. *I could never have left her. Who could?*

Hunter put the phone down. Help would arrive. Now he had to finish what he'd started: protect her, save her—whatever that meant now.

"I didn't exactly kill him," Olivia mused.

"What do you mean by *exactly*?"

"I gave clear instructions. Get back in his car and drive as fast as he could." She flicked her hair like it was nothing.

Hunter turned the key and eased the car off the curb. They coasted past the wreckage. Neighbors spilled from a nearby hotel, shrieking as they realized how narrowly they'd been spared.

Blue and red lights flickered in the rearview mirror, fading behind them. Olivia sprawled back, legs up, dirty feet pressed to the window, humming happily, her knees bouncing with each note.

9

———

CHAPTER NINE.

"Your tree," Olivia's ethereal yet eerie voice seeped into Hunter's bones, "is not thriving."

Hunter slid his thick skeleton key into his front door, hearing the heavy click as he turned it. She stood behind him, goosebumps prickling her arms while she lingered. Olivia blinked at the withering bare tree in his front yard.

Hunter was about to invite her into the home he and Sarah had built together. A place of peace and refuge that would now be a refuge for something more violent.

Are you really saving her?

"It's just winter," he mumbled, opening the front door and stepping into his home. "All the trees look like this when it's cold."

"Not the trees in the forest," she replied. "They thrive in all seasons."

Hunter waited for a sign, an omen of anger from Sarah's ghost, before he stepped inside and let Olivia in. It felt like a betrayal, bringing a woman here who collected his stares, whose lips had stolen his breath.

A horrifying feeling crept into his heart, the certainty that once her toes touched his floor, nothing would ever be the same. He could never turn back.

But no omen came.

She's only a guest. You're being paranoid.

Though when Olivia's near-naked body was bent over his in the car, no thoughts of her being "only" anything had crossed his mind. He hoped his silent prayer to any spirit listening would count for something.

Because he cared.

He cared so much that the ache it caused could not heal. There would be no recovery.

Besides, Sarah's ghost wouldn't haunt you. She would watch over you.

Olivia stepped inside behind him as he reached out to pull the cord on the lamp, illuminating the living room, scaring away the shadows that lurked. Shadows that Hunter assumed would watch with curiosity as this new monster had found herself with his crushed spirit effortlessly woven around her.

His situation felt precarious as he turned to her, the digital clock above the mantle glowing bright crimson.

3:46 a.m.

"It isn't much," Hunter said, but Olivia held out her hand and hushed him as she took in the room. She gasped and giggled when the clock changed to the next minute. The sound was infectious, and Hunter found himself laughing, too.

It was a nervous, misplaced chuckle because there was no denying that his world was not her world. The modern day was so new, so foreign to her.

Her large, dark eyes devoured every detail.

"It's everything," she exhaled, staring at him like he was something important.

Hunter cleared his throat to break the spell. How easy this was, standing with her.

"We need to work on empathy a bit, but you're welcome to

stay for as long as you need. I'll sleep on the couch. The bedroom is just down the hallway."

"My empathy?"

"That cop didn't deserve that."

"Oh, right, because it's Christmas." Olivia sighed, as if Hunter was ruining her joy.

"You only have the one bedroom?"

"There are two. The other one is used for storage... hobbies, I guess."

"Hobbies?"

"Painting, knitting, I think there are some pottery supplies in there too."

"The home I grew up in had many rooms."

Ritzy little tree siren, I see.

"Vultauge Manor, I know it well," he replied.

Olivia's head snapped to him at the name, her mouth frowning.

"What did I say?" he asked.

"My family name. I almost forgot it." She left it at that.

Hunter moved into his bedroom, the worn beige carpet under his feet. He slid the mirrored closet door open and crouched in the back, pulling out a box. It was a box that he had never opened, not since he had packed it.

Sarah's clothes.

Hunter couldn't bear to get rid of them or give them to her family. He swore her citrus perfume still lingered, though maybe that was only in his head after all these years.

There were sweatpants inside and a warm thermal shirt. Getting Olivia clothed before she slept in Sarah's bed, in their bed, felt necessary.

He frowned at the black heavy metal band t-shirt he picked up, thinking about the piece of clothing on another woman.

This is wrong.

He wouldn't do it. He wouldn't mix memories like this.

Hunter put the shirt back into the box and tucked it away. It was better sealed away, safe from time and air that would one day steal any lingering scent. The thought made his stomach sink.

"I can work with the tree," Olivia said, running her hand along the bedspread, the frame, the pillows. "Would that make up for the cop? I would be happy to make it happy."

Hunter stood, grabbing one of his t-shirts stuffed on the bottom shelf of his closet, followed by a pair of jersey shorts that fit him too snugly. He waited for guilt to hit him, to feel the blood on her hands staining his too. It never came, and that scared him more.

Where is your panic, Hunter?

"Here, you can wear this tonight. I'll show you how the shower works in the morning," he said, closing the distance between them and handing her the clothes.

Olivia stepped closer to him, letting the jacket she wore fall to the floor. The clothes crumpled between their bodies as she stared into his eyes, not smiling, not grimacing, but there was a light, a spark that flashed in her pupils.

"Your eyes," he said. Lustrous, intoxicating, Hunter found himself falling into them again and again. Hot frothy espresso in a mug to greet him after being too long in the cold, ready to wrap him in warmth, in a blanket of terror and comfort, horror and kisses.

"What about them?" she breathed.

Hunter took a step back.

"You asked me what I saw in the car. It was a black hole in the ground; vines inched out, reaching, growing, threatening to swallow everything near. It felt like they were looking for me—the vines, the emptiness."

"Hmmm." She smiled, aloof, her gaze moving toward the ceiling as she got lost in the world that only existed in her mind. Her body bobbled, her eyelids fell closed, and she raised her chin as if she were standing in the middle of a field during a summer rainstorm. It was as if she were absorbing the environment around her, the stillness of the ceiling, and the light rapping of the wind on the shutters outside. "Maybe they were."

Olivia grabbed the clothes out of his hands with the speed of a cat, raising the shirt to her face in confusion. It would engulf her.

"Why do I have to wear this?"

"Because I'd expect more propriety from a woman born in the early nineteen hundreds," Hunter said.

Olivia laughed in his face, her smile big and beautiful, filled with the light he would expect to see bouncing off a waterfall deep in a Scottish forest.

"It's easy to forget that I'm not one of them," she admitted.

"One of them?"

"One of the trees."

Hunter put his hands over hers, gently removing the shirt. She let him, her arms dropping to her sides and waiting while he opened it from the bottom.

"Arms up," he instructed, and she obeyed.

He slid the shirt over her head, getting her hands through the appropriate holes.

"Are trees quite scandalous then?" he smirked at his sarcasm.

"Oh yes," she said thoughtfully. "You'd be surprised at their thoughts, communications, and rage."

"Rage?" Hunter asked.

"Would you not have rage if you were a tree?"

He hadn't thought about it.

Why would you think about it?

"Olivia," Hunter said softly, opening the shorts as she stepped into them. "Can you explain again? Why did you leave the forest?"

"I thought that was clear," she mused, now covered, the

shorts barely hanging onto her hips. "You sang for me. No one's ever sung to the trees like that before, no one's ever come back and sung then, just for me."

Hunter ruffled the back of his hair nervously.

"It's not a traditionally manly trait, singing." He laughed awkwardly, turning around. "But I used to sing to myself in the middle of the night as a kid. When I woke up scared, my parents' bedroom was far on the other side of a hallway. In the night, it felt like that hallway led somewhere else."

He got lost in the memory, lost in that too-large house with the people that were supposed to protect him so far from reach.

Olivia hummed, bringing him back.

"Let me know if you need help figuring out the bed. I'll grab one of these pillows here. I'll be out in the living room."

He could have sworn that the vines on the windowsill shivered, stretching ever so slightly toward him as he bid her goodnight.

10

CHAPTER TEN.

Knock. Knock. Knock.

The first set of bangs on the door woke Hunter from his sleep, but instead of standing and running to the door, he struggled to open his eyes. Heat from the sunlight streaming in through his single-pane windows warmed his chin. His body sank into the cushions, the ribbed fabric of the couch rubbing against his right hip as his shirt shifted out of place, an innocent betrayal.

Knock. Knock. Knock.

Who would come here so early?

"Go away," he muttered, knowing no one could hear him.

"Hunter Nethanial Gunnan," a shrill woman's voice came from the other side of the front door. "I have a key, and I will use it."

Mom.

"She'll do it, son. Time to get decent."

Dad.

Hunter sprang up off the pillow and blanket, which tangled around his feet and tripped him. He wobbled forward, trying not to trip, but it was too late. The click of the latch sounded, and the front door swung open, bringing in the chill from outside and the most frightening thing that could appear in his home at that time: his parents.

"Are you still in bed?" He could hear his mom's voice, the heels in her boots thudding with her short, bouncy steps. They carried her straight down the hallway, into his bedroom.

"A woman!" she screamed.

There it is.

"Oh, I'm so sorry. I'm here looking for my son. He lives here. You've got such pretty hair."

"I found him," his dad called, standing in the entryway to the living room. "Over here, Minerva."

Dad, still unfairly handsome for his sixties, clapped Hunter's back like nothing was out of place. The full head of silver hair, the stubble, the cheap clothes—everything exactly the same as always.

People said Hunter looked like him. He hoped they were right.

His mom marched in with the energy of the fifth graders in his class. Her bleached blonde hair was pinned tight, and pearls dangled from her ears. Her bright red jacket tapered down to her knees to show off her black boots.

"Mark, there's a girl in Hunter's room."

"I heard, Minerva," his dad sighed. "Hunter, there's a woman in your bed."

"Oh my gosh, I am so proud of you," Mom threw her arms around Hunter's neck, forcing him to bend down a few inches. She pulled his face close to hers.

"I loved Sarah. We all did, but it's only healthy to have a rebound."

"Mom . . ." Hunter groaned. "Dad, a little help here?"

"I'll be staying out of this one," Dad said, flopping onto the couch and pulling out his phone.

"Wait a minute." Mom looked down at the bedding thrown

across the floor. "Did you sleep on the couch? Mark, he slept on the couch."

"Have you made any coffee yet?" his dad asked him, knees cracking as he stood right back up. Hunter shook his head. "I'll go start a pot."

"The woman in my bed, Mom," Hunter started, "is a friend who needed help. She was in some trouble. Her name is Olivia."

The eyebrows drawn on his mom's face defied gravity. "What kind of trouble?"

"It doesn't matter. It's personal stuff. I'm just trying to be a good guy."

"You're the best guy," his mom said, coming in for another hug.

"Did you hear about the accident in town?" his dad yelled from the kitchen, cabinets slamming as he dug for supplies.

"Ground beans are on the counter in the tin," Hunter answered. "And what accident?"

"A police car ran into the general store last night, right on Market Street. The officer died. I could only assume drugs. Some world we live in these days."

Hunter's breath left his body. It was becoming a habit.

Olivia entered the living room. Her hair had been disheveled before, but now it had the extra bedhead texture. Her clothes swallowed her. Still, magic surrounded her—there was no denying a special kind of beauty.

"Oh, my dear." Hunter's mom turned towards her, taking Olivia's hands, looking at the bruises, at the scratches on her skin. "What you must have been through. Your feet are nearly black with dirt. This won't do. Let's go get you in the shower. Hunter, why hasn't she gotten a hot bath?"

Hunter didn't know how to react; the last time Olivia was around another person, they'd ended up dead.

She's dangerous. She's holding Mom's hands, blood on her own skin. You brought her here.

Maybe he was grumpy from the lack of sleep, or maybe more levelheaded after some hours had passed, but when Hunter looked at Olivia, he felt fear and uncertainty.

"It was late, Mom," Hunter answered, "when we got in."

"You poor thing, you must be traumatized to look like this. Let me help you." His mom pulled Olivia away, and she smiled at him but went willingly. She was quiet today, around all the new people she had unfortunately woken up to.

It was easy to clear his head when he wasn't staring into her eyes. That warmth could make him forget everything else.

Hunter listened to his mom fuss over Olivia, her high-pitched voice coming through the closed bathroom door down the hallway.

"Not too hot, dear, you just step in. Oh my gosh, you are too skinny—we need to get some food in you. What must you have been through? My Hunter is such a saint."

"Mom, leave Olivia alone." Hunter put his head between his hands and flopped back onto the couch, groaning. He wouldn't put it past his mom to jump into the shower with her and help her wash her hair.

The comforting smell of cheap coffee filled his nostrils as his dad came out of the kitchen, placing a beige mug on the low square glass living room table a few feet before him.

"You have no idea how much joy your mom is getting out of you having a new friend," his dad said, sitting next to him, sipping his coffee. "Too hot."

"Why are you guys here without a text, Dad?" Hunter asked. "Didn't we talk about boundaries?"

Mark chuckled, spilling some coffee on his hand. "Ouch. Can't catch a break."

Hunter lifted his head and looked over at the man who raised him.

"Your teacher friend, Sadie, texted your mom yesterday, concerned." Mark put his coffee on the table only to rummage around in his jacket pocket, pulling out a crumpled paper.

"Of course she did."

"It's been years, son." He slapped the paper on the table, splashing coffee. "We all miss Sarah. I don't know who this woman is or why she is here, but you need this."

"Define *this*." Hunter stared at the paper revealed. It was a folded check. "Dad, who even writes checks anymore?"

"I'm too old for change now." Mark chuckled. "And when I say this, I mean change. I mean something new. I can't be your only friend, as much as I love you, son. And hell, even if that's my fate, I'd love to come over here without having to smell vinegar."

"Sorry, I barely notice the smell anymore."

"She doesn't even have any clothes. Where is this poor girl from?" His mom's voice shrilled through the house, her footsteps determined as she exited through the front door.

Hunter shook his head, and his father laughed.

"Why don't you sell those pickles at a farmers' market? You could meet new people there."

"I have another friend, Dad. She texts you about my well-being, so you show up unannounced. Please put that check back in your pocket. I don't need it."

His father sighed. "I'll just leave it right there. Tear it up after I go if I must."

The two let silence pass between them as they sipped too-hot coffee, trying not to flinch.

The front door opened again, and his mom huffed and puffed down the hallway to the bathroom.

"That woman cannot be stopped." Mark laughed before slapping Hunter's left shoulder. "We just worry. It's our job, I suppose."

"I know, Dad. Thanks."

With that, Mark stood up, his knees cracking, running his hands through his gorgeous head of hair.

"Minvera, we should leave the kids to be kids," Mark bellowed.

"Almost done," Hunter's mom rang out like a school bell ringing over a hangover.

Hunter grimaced. "I should go check on them."

"What can happen? You've got to let ladies do what ladies do."

Hunter imagined walking into the bathroom, his mom wrapped in vines, her eyes lifeless.

Don't leave your mom to be butchered, you idiot.

He jumped to his feet. Mark very much noticed the sudden panic.

"What did I say?" his dad asked, following him with wide, quick strides down the hall.

His hallways were framed by the same wooden slats that were installed in the 1970s remodel by the owners two generations back. Hunter's feet stopped mid-step as the bathroom door opened, and relief rushed in as Minvera came bouncing out into the hall. The smile on her face was one of a plan gone right, but Hunter looked past that for now.

"I pulled some clothes from the car, just some basics that I would be donating, so don't sweat it. Hunter, your girl is so stunning."

His mom squealed and squeezed Hunter's shoulders while his dad lingered at the back of the hallway, hands in his pockets, dying to leave.

"We are only friends, Mom. I'm sorry to break your heart."

"I've got a few more things to get out of the trunk. I'll leave you crazy kids to yourselves. Come help me, Mark!"

With his mom already behind him, Hunter raised his chin to greet Olivia, who emerged slowly, cautiously, from the small and cramped bathroom.

"I ... you ... wow," Hunter stammered, his palms fumbling with the collar of his t-shirt, not knowing what to do with them.

He knew, however, what he wanted to do with them.

She's yours.

Olivia's black, thick hair was lustrous, shining like glitter in a snow globe from the fluorescent lights above. Hunter didn't even realize he had a hair dryer, and decided that yes, his mom would be the type to drive around with one as he peeped at the large square brush and dark green hand tool sitting still plugged in on the bathroom sink.

The earthy smell that had entranced him before was still there, lingering beneath whatever fragrance came out of his two-in-one shampoo. He assumed it was the pink flowers that were displayed on the bottle.

"Your first shower in one hundred years?"

That's your opening line, huh?

Olivia raised her thick, dark eyebrows at him. He imagined a bright red apple against her lips, freshly washed with droplets skidding down the fruit onto her chin.

The contrast of colors, the brightness against her milky white skin.

Your. Girl.

Hunter was not the possessive alpha male type, no gym rat, no six-pack. He was a normal guy, a grieving guy, a sometimes funny, quirky guy who had enough common sense to run away from monsters. But here, he was staring into her eyes, inhaling deeply as he tried to memorize her scent. As he tried to figure out how he could become a part of it.

You're gone.

Sarah, I'm losing my mind.

He had thought that to himself too often these past few days.

Olivia wasn't going anywhere. He couldn't let her go.

You sound ridiculous.

"It was warmer than the rain," Olivia whispered, her hollow cheeks almost pinching, a secret dimple threatening to appear.

"The clothes fit well," Hunter murmured, unable to stop his eyes from drifting down her slight frame. The spell she carried wrapped around him all over again. It was not magic now. Just Olivia and him. His stomach tightened; his lips parted.

Olivia wore a long, thick sweater dress, black to match her hair and eyes. It fell down to her calves, paired with chunky, shiny boots.

"It suits you, really," he said softly while she tucked her hair behind her ear.

"I'm baaaaa-ack," his mom announced. Hunter watched her pass him in the hallway with an armful of plants.

"Don't just stand there, help me," his mom barked at a helpless Mark.

"Yes, ma'am," his dad grumbled, stepping aside.

"Should we help? Unless you'd rather be alone?" Hunter asked, glancing at Olivia and lifting his hand to signal she should walk first. Olivia's long eyelashes nearly brushed her cheeks as she blinked, that smile still lingering, carved soft but sharp. A perfect, flawless, wicked doll.

She moved, walking down the hallway in front of him, her head turning over her shoulder to scan him slowly. He would kill to know what that look meant, what she was thinking. The dress hugged her frame, her waist so slender, yet her hips swished back and forth, like a salsa dancer at center stage.

Is she doing that on purpose?

Olivia looked over her shoulder again, her smirk confirming it. Hunter raised an eyebrow at her as they turned into the living room, where his mom was fussing over seven potted poinsettias.

"Mom," Hunter huffed. "Why?"

"Oh, you insult me, Hunter. Christmas is in six days, and

you would have never known it by stepping into this joyless house."

That's because Sarah isn't here. She was the cheer.

"And since you refuse to visit home, where it is properly—"

"Extravagantly," his dad cut in, earning a look from his wife that promised that he would pay for that later.

"Properly decorated," she continued, "I thought I'd bring some of that holiday spirit here."

"Mom, is this because of Sadie's text? There is nothing to worry about. Besides, this is too much. Where am I supposed to put all of these?"

"Oh, nonsense." His mom tapped Hunter on his shoulder, a too-large smile pinned across her face. "Olivia here can help you, I'm sure. A fun little project that might make your home smell better."

Olivia reached in between a few of the poinsettia's red blooms, pulling out a sprig of mistletoe, pale berries nestled among the sharp green.

"Well, I've got to go donate those items to the church. You know how the ladies get when I'm late."

"We don't go to church," his dad grunted, earning another glare.

"I have to donate it somewhere, Mark. I love you, pumpkin. Have a good day. Mark, we are going," she yelled even though his dad stood right beside her.

Hunter glanced at Olivia, who seemed half amused, half lost in thought as she turned the sprig between her fingers.

"Thank you for your kindness," Olivia called after his mom. The woman turned and gave her a wink.

"Those crazy kids," he heard his mom mutter with glee as the two exited. Hunter and Olviia were alone again as the cold wind violently slammed the door shut.

"How different parents are in this time," Olivia murmured, lifting the mistletoe higher, inspecting its leaves.

"I'm sorry about them. I wasn't expecting . . ."

Any of this.

She turned to face him fully. "What an interesting plant to bring. It's very up front about how it's poisonous; its jarring red warning signs are ignored, and instead, it gets worshiped as holiday decor."

Olivia spoke to the poinsettias then, "Don't worry, little ones, I'm here."

11

CHAPTER ELEVEN.

It was hard to leave Olivia alone, even if he was just down the hall. Hunter returned to the living room feeling refreshed, dressed for whatever surprises awaited him now.

Olivia was in his living room unsupervised. Hunter chewed on his thumbnail until he gave up and went to check on her.

With fresh socks, his thicker snow pants, and a hoodie, Hunter stood under the entryway, staring at Olivia's back, as she sang to the plants his mom left behind, her voice light, hushed as if she were telling them secrets.

She probably is.

The stress that had pulsed through him—while he dressed with the urgency of an Olympic speed skater—began to fade. His heartbeat slowed as her song wrapped around his head, seeping into his blood. It was a haze, a poison he'd drink willingly.

His mind, drunk on the moment, whispered that nothing had ever felt so right. Not with her there, wistful and glowing, mistletoe held just shy of her lips.

There was no question—Hunter saw it move.

The mistletoe twitched, softened, seemed to breathe in her hands. Its leaves curled and relaxed, responding to her song the same way his body did.

But unlike him, it didn't just react. It grew.

New life unfurled—leaves the deepest shade of green, berries a vivid crimson—spilling out from the original six-inch stem she'd held delicately between her fingers.

Hunter took it all in, awe oozing out of his pores. The leaves had reached the floor, falling in small circles like rope, a vine of thick, pointed holiday cheer.

The unbelievably soul-crushing beauty of her siren song stopped.

"That's enough for now," Olivia said to the vine. "Now, where to hang you where light can shine through the windows?" She turned, her face pensive, her lips pursed and pulled to the side.

Adorable.

His head was stuck in that haze, the spell from her song. He knew he didn't need it; his thoughts of her were true, but it did help erase the anxiety that hid in his stomach, knowing what she could do, knowing it was likely just a part of what magic she had.

"I'd like to wrap this around the mantle." She didn't ask, as if this were her house.

"You can decorate however you wish," he said, bowing slightly.

Bowed. You bowed.

A full smile spread across Olivia's face, her nose scrunching a little. The confidence his approval gave her sent butterflies into a vortex formation inside his core. He smiled back as she skipped over to the mantle, placing what she could carry of the elongated mistletoe along the back, humming and coaxing the plant into hanging. It grew and slid into several feet of corkscrew-shaped vines, hanging onto the textured walls in the living room once there was no room left.

After a few blinks, yards of green graced the entire living room, wrapping around the beamed ceiling overhead.

"Wow," Hunter said, "the house is already so different."

He knew that the forest responded to her voice, her song, but seeing the magic that laced her vocal cords in action with natural light in a familiar space was a new level of surreal. Hunter stared at her in awe, doing his best not to allow his mouth to hang open.

"It's filled with life now," she whispered.

Hunter's mood plummeted, triggered by the words from the lips he so carefully studied.

Life.

Like when Sarah was alive.

It was a sobering sentence, uttered from the first woman he felt pulled to get to know since the tragedy. The haze of Olivia's song did what it could to push the grief out of his mind, focusing him only on this black-haired beauty, but Hunter couldn't allow himself to forget. He would never forget.

Am I ready for this? If she wants me, too, can I move forward, Sarah?

"What are your hobbies?" The question felt small, but it tugged him out of the quiet cocoon of his grief.

Smooth, Romeo.

Olivia only blinked at him, her smile waning. "Hobbies?"

"What did you do for fun before you went into the forest, before you decided to never come back out?"

"You want to know me, Hunter?" Her head tilted, considering. "Is that why you sang for me?"

She's crazy and terrifying; why can't I let her go?

He nodded.

"What is this box?" she asked, moving her finger across the dusty screen.

"It's called a TV, a television. It plays stories that move. Should I turn it on?"

Olivia frowned at it and shook her head no. "Your tree doesn't like it."

"My tree outside?" Hunter looked out the window.

"It doesn't like the noise. Its hum is too loud when the sun goes down."

"I didn't realize."

Who would?

"I don't think I had any hobbies. I worked in my little garden, the one my mother had made for me under the window to my bedroom," she finally answered his question. "When I was sure that I was alone, I would sing to the plants— the jasmine, the pink alliums, the lavender, and the thick vines that grew up the side of the brick. It was the only time I was allowed to sing, when there was no one there to hear."

Hunter looked for sadness in his eyes, but he only saw acceptance.

"I studied with my tutor," she continued. "I went to dance lessons. I was regularly fitted for new dresses as I tore mine running barefoot. I was always purposely losing the strings to my corsets."

Olivia's focus moved on to the coffee table that was still alive with the seven poinsettia plants. Hunter winced, just a little, imagining the house filled with hundreds of them if she took the same route with the festive red leaves as she had with the mistletoe.

He supposed it could be funny, explaining to the neighborhood that his little house exploded from wild holiday plants.

Your willingness to accept that was awfully fast, Hunter.

Olivia held her hand out over the leaves, petting them, and like a cat, Hunter swore he could almost hear it purr back at her. She hummed, the leaves curling under in response, comforted, nurtured, the red color brightening even more. Hunter had never seen a natural color so brilliant.

"Where should we put them?" Hunter asked.

"They are asking for more light," she said. "The poor things have been practically deprived, but still bloom to the best of their ability. They are valiant, strong." She lowered her voice, speaking to the plants, "I'm proud of you all."

There was no tune to her voice, but the plants still reacted, shooting up, each growing four or five feet, nearly tumbling over as the shiny gold foil paper that held their plastic container crinkled with ferocity. Olivia beamed at them, her children.

Hunter put his hands on his face and bent, crouched down to brace himself. There was no silence once the foil stopped resisting, no cracking of the containers that split down the middle, no dirt flooding the floor. Instead, his ears were immediately hit with an uncontrollable, free laughter. Hunter looked up at Olivia, partially hidden by the foliage surrounding her. Her hands were on her belly, and her face was pointed at the ceiling as her body shook from joy.

Hunter wasn't sure if he should be offended or not.

You probably should.

"I didn't know what was going to happen," he said, and stood awkwardly, rubbing the back of his neck, grimacing.

"Are you scared of me, Hunter?" she asked, and the laughter finally ran out of her body like helium being squeezed from a balloon. The energy was lighter; there was a joy in his living room that wasn't there before, that hadn't existed in any way.

"Terrified, if we are being honest." He chuckled.

It wasn't a lie.

"I think I rather enjoy that." She tenderly moved her hands through the poinsettias that now stood at her eye level. "I suppose we could move them in front of each window. They will need larger pots. Do you have any to spare?"

Hunter shook his head, bewildered that he would be expected to have such a thing lying around.

Maybe for her, you should.

"I can get some. I can go now if you'd like. I can bring back some takeout, too."

"Take out?" Olivia cocked her head.

"Food prepared in a kitchen, a restaurant," he clarified. "Catering, perhaps."

She nodded.

"What kind of food did you eat in the forest?"

"I stood in the rain, I soaked up the moisture from the soil, I pulled in vitamins from the sunshine when I dipped my toes out of the edges of the trees."

You're going to make this as hard as possible for me.

"Olivia, what did you like to eat before you became a part of the bark?"

"Hmmmm." She smiled. "I don't remember eating much. I was always a bit of a waif as a child. I suppose that I appreciated sweets and beautiful pastries that were displayed near the champagne fountains on birthdays and during balls."

"During Christmas?" Hunter asked.

She nodded again.

"If I leave to get sturdy pots for the poinsettias, will the house still be standing when I return?"

Olivia smirked. "Perhaps."

"How does it work?" Hunter asked. "The plants grew without you singing. You only spoke to them that time."

"They are a part of me; I am a part of them. My singing is necessary only to control other humans, a funny consequence."

"Is it just men that are affected?"

"That's a peculiar question. Plants do not have genders."

Hunter sighed. "Your singing—does it only work on men? Or does everyone forget?"

"Women are affected as well."

Hunter walked into the kitchen, turning his back on her to grab his wallet off the counter. When he returned, Olivia was peering out the front window, her eyes large, sad.

"Your poor tree," she whispered.

"We can put the TV in the garage, unplugged when I return," he suggested.

"Yes, we must. We must bring it relief."

Hunter opened the front door and walked out of the house. "I'll be right back. Please stay inside, don't talk to anyone, don't trust anyone."

Olivia just stared at the tree from the window, blowing her hair off of her face, her eyes going vacant as she sighed.

Hunter closed the door, watching her from the other side of the window, his stomach tightening again as he admired her face, her hair, her beauty, her strangeness.

"Let's go buy pots on your teacher's salary," he muttered to himself as he walked to his car, the snow on his lawn crunching under his boots.

12

CHAPTER TWELVE.

"That one," Hunter said to the jolly middle-aged man behind the counter, his face too close to the glass as he stared at the pastries on the other side.

"Good choice, that's one of our specialties for the season," the man said, grabbing the beige fluffy pastry topped with powdered sugar and candied oranges.

Hunter didn't often explore the more tourist-focused shops on Main Street, but the nearest nursery in Stockbridge was only a few blocks away, and he was famished. If sweets were what soothed the tree siren's stomach, then they would eat like kings today.

"Are you Klaus?" Hunter pointed to the wall sign, the store named Klaus's Danish Bakery in bright, cheery letters. The man behind the counter lit up, his jolly cheeks perfect cherry circles, nodding enthusiastically.

"I am. It's a busy season, so all hands on deck this week. We've got more than three hundred Kransekages to make before customers come in to pick them up for their holiday celebrations."

"That's amazing. This place is so great, though maybe not

so great for my wallet," Hunter said, pointing to another donut-like Danish topped with berries and cream.

"How many?" Klaus asked, chuckling.

"Let's get two of those as well."

Klaus wrapped eight Danishes in a creamy cerulean box and tied them with a beige string. "Let's get these in your car before the rain starts," Klaus said, watching Hunter insert his credit card into the reader.

He looked out the glass windows to see the dark gray skies inching overhead.

"Nothing cozier than snuggling up on a rainy day and eating Danishes. Sharing them with someone special?"

Hunter took the box Klaus held out to him. "You could say that."

"Judging by the blush on your face, I'd take a guess that they are really special."

Hunter didn't have the heart to tell Klaus that his face was red from the blistering cold winds whipping at his face as he walked the block to the storefront. Besides, he could be lying to himself. Olivia could only be described as special.

"She is," Hunter finally said, waving and exiting the store. The ring of the gold bell above the door bid him farewell as he hurried to his car.

Hunter set the box on the passenger seat floor, wincing as his elbow knocked against a black, glossy pot jutting from the backseat. It wasn't alone. Three more crowded beside it, heavy and awkward, their bulk promising an unpleasant struggle once he got home. One rogue pot had already escaped to the trunk, rolling and thumping with every turn. Each distant thud spiked his pulse as he waited to hear one shatter and break.

Part of him hoped Olivia was still at the window, staring out at the tree in his yard. It had been so long since he'd come home to someone, and the thought alone stirred small butter-flies deep in his stomach.

But coming through Market Street today had reminded him of the cost of ignoring warnings. The general store was boarded up now, caution cones and tape forcing pedestrians to weave around it—a silent memorial. Flowers wilted in the cold, hand-painted signs faded by the season, and stuffed toys sagged under melting snow, all a tribute to the fallen officer.

The Mason family had no answers. And they never would. Only he and Olivia knew and ever would know.

She's a murderer, and you don't care. She's a murderer, and you didn't turn her in.

Of course, he cared. He cared about her too much. That scared him. It shook him to his core. It was so right, mysterious, and because of his never-ending grief, because of the lifeless person he had morphed into in the past few years, this all felt wrong. A woman who piqued his interest, made him curious, was filled with every red flag possible, a nurturing that couldn't be pure evil.

She was scared once, too. The nonchalant sinisterness that rose to the surface, gleaming from her eyes in sneaky one-second intervals, only existed because she was once fighting for something. Isn't that how all villain origin stories began? He'd have to see if his comic book collection was still in that box in his parents' attic.

She could not like you. She could be using you.

Hunter could not get past the thought, a blinding archway inviting him into the world that was Olivia. He would go through it, protecting his heart, protecting Sarah's memory, keeping his distance while continuing to be a gentleman.

She's yours.

Hunter laughed out loud at his own jumbled, contradicting thoughts. The car moved forward with his foot pressing against the gas pedal, wheels spinning on slush and ice until he pulled back out onto the salted, snow-plowed road. He got stuck behind a car going fifteen miles under the speed limit as the clouds opened up, letting the rain drizzle down, a light mist that would get heavier as he gripped the steering wheel and tried to control his road rage.

We live in Massachusetts—how can you be scared to drive in the weather?

When he finally made it and turned down his street, the rain had progressed into a violent dumping. His windshield wipers struggled to catch up. Hunter let out a yelp, swerving the car, stepping on the brakes in panic when he noticed a figure standing in the middle of the road, nearly blending in with the rain, with the doom and gloom of the day.

He opened his car door and let out his frustrations.

"What the heck are you doing? Are you trying to get killed, you idiot?"

"Your tree is so melancholy that it called on the sky to cry, to ask for attention."

Olivia.

Hunter's eyes quickly looked over to his house, only a few lots down, to make sure it was still standing. It looked the same from where he stood. The tree was also unchanged. The front door was wide open, the rain spilling onto his already damaged, old wooden flooring.

Olivia was soaked from head to toe, the thick sweater dress retaining water that streamed off a seam on her thigh. She didn't shiver despite the bluish tone to her cheeks; she only smiled as she tilted her head back, letting her arms stretch wide as she began to turn and dance.

"What are you doing?" he asked, walking towards her, his car in park but still running, the engine purring under the sound of heavy droplets against metal, against the pavement, and houses around them.

"You reminded me that I was hungry," she shouted, spinning, swaying, water puddling at her feet while she kicked and stomped with elation. She hummed, and Hunter watched as the trees and bushes in yards nearby seemed to lean in towards her, as if they were waiting for something.

"In this world," he said, putting his hand out and gripping her by the arm, "we don't get our nutrients from the rain."

Olivia stopped moving, her smile wiped as she looked down at his hand gripping her.

"Everything grows because of rain."

"I'm sorry," he said, letting go. He'd gotten lost in the moment, casually touching her like they had known each other their entire lives. "I wasn't thinking, I just wanted to get you into the warmth."

Instead of pulling away, Olivia shuffled in towards him, her fingers finding his as she raised them, two star-shaped hands, wet, cold palms touching. Hunter curved his fingers in, intertwining with hers as rain dripped off his nose, soaking through his coat, his pants.

He could still smell her, even in the downpour. That warm earth smell brought him relief, any worry he had going away, as if her song were casting a spell over him again. This time, there was no song, no haze. There were only the deep, dark eyes that stared into his, that bore into his soul. It was as if she had been waiting one hundred years for him.

"Where else can I absorb more nutrients?" she asked.

Was she breathless? Panting under her words?

Or was that him?

Olivia pulled her hands down to her sides, bringing his with her as she came into him, no more space separating them, her chest pressing against his, her chin raising to his. Hunter succumbed to how she felt against him, how he was putty in her hands. He surrendered. There was no going back after this. Hunter placed his lips on hers. This kiss was something new. It felt like electricity zapping him as he stood in a puddle.

She's yours.

It was as if it were the very first, a kiss that confirmed he was choosing to be a different man, a different person. This kiss would ensure that he needed to take action, be proactive, and take care of the beautiful, strange creature that trusted him enough to follow him into a world that was not hers.

She baited him, staring at him with those longing, thick, wet eyelashes, inviting him in. She wanted that kiss, too. She wanted him. She saw something in him. Olivia saw something that he himself could not see. Whatever it was, he could learn, change, and become better. He could bring that out of himself and let the entire world see that he got a second chance, that Hunter was worthy of life.

You can do this. You can move on.

Their lips pulled apart. Hunter smiled, his cheeks heated, his heart open as he stared into the danger he could not escape.

She needed him.

He needed her.

It was that simple.

"I'm not sure that filled me." Olivia smirked.

Hunter wasted no time. He needed no more of an invitation as his hand moved to the back of her head, her wet hair still silky but tangling at his aggressive movement. He crushed his lips to her as their momentum built, as their mouths moved together, a tango that was desperate, dark, but so fulfilling that Hunter might never be able to come back up for air again.

A light moan came out of Olivia which sent Hunter into a spiral, a frenzy as he worried that he might devour hers right there in the middle of the street, in the puddle that they stood in as neighbors peered through their windows and watched as for the first time in years, Hunter came alive, found himself once more, found himself in her.

Honk Honk Honk

Olivia jumped up while still entangled in their kiss, and he held her tighter, closer, protectively as their lips broke. Hunter looked to the left to see an angry elderly woman sitting in her car, unable to get around his vehicle in the single-lane residential street.

"You're bothering people." She rolled her window down, shouting through heavy rain. "Move your car."

Olivia giggled, and Hunter could breathe, breaking free from the moment that had wrapped around them.

"I'm sorry," he said, holding a hand up to her. "Come sit in the car with me; I have to park."

The two marched through pools of water on the pavement, Hunter sitting in the driver's seat just in time to watch Olivia's surprised face as she nearly stepped on the box of Danishes on the floor.

Hunter grabbed the box, holding it with his right hand over the center console so she could sit, and began to pull the car into his driveway. The rain had melted away most of the snow as the unhappy woman sped by unnecessarily fast.

"Look at these pots," Olivia said, her face lighting up. "You got these for me?"

"Yes, and that's not all," Hunter said, opening the Danish box. "I got some nutrients. Well, health bloggers will argue that these aren't nutrients, but I hope you like them anyway."

"Health bloggers?" She blinked at them, a bit confused, but there was no denying the elation beaming through her, as if she were trying to summon the sun.

13

CHAPTER THIRTEEN.

Olivia hummed softly as she cradled the oversized poinsettia, gently teasing its roots apart before settling it into the soil Hunter poured into the oversized planter pot in the living room. The haze that crept into Hunter's mind was less and less intrusive, as if it recognized him as a friend and was no longer looking for its next victim.

He was sore from carrying multiple forty-pound planter pots and a few bags of loose soil from the car. He successfully held his breath so Olivia didn't see evidence of his lack of gym time.

You're getting there in age. People throw their backs out doing this kind of work, Hunter.

The rich scent of earth surrounded him, mingling with the light bite of herbs coming from the mistletoe hung throughout the living room, draping as if it had a personality, determined to be elegant and dramatic. His entire house now had her scent wafting through as if she had touched every fabric and piece of furniture. It smelled like forest. It smelled like trees. It smelled like her body was pressed against him. Her body pressed so close, without rain to wash her away, and him desperate to hold on.

Hunter blushed and looked down into the fresh dirt sitting like a bowl inside the three feet of shiny porcelain pot in front of his main living room window. The bag that once held the soil lay crumpled against the front door, making a mess he would have to clean up later.

The thought of Olivia rolling around, rolling around with him, was now all he could think about.

Get a hold of yourself. It was just a kiss.

But maybe it wasn't. Maybe it was fate itself. Maybe it was the permission he had longed for after all these years, the permission to be free.

The heavy rain turned into hail, the light pattering on the roof suddenly violent, brazen. Olivia froze, a deer in the headlights, eyes wide and unblinking.

"I can turn poisonous," she said, her voice hushed.

"What?" Hunter rocked back on his heel, unsure if he should laugh or be scared.

"We are being attacked, or can you not hear that as well?"

"Olivia," Hunter breathed, realizing what was happening. "It's hail. It's freezing rain. Have you never seen that before?"

She seemed unsure.

"No, that's not it," he said. "You just haven't been under a roof for a very long time. Don't worry, this is how it sounds—"

"When the sky throws down ice," she cut him off. He nodded.

"Did you say you're poisonous?" he asked.

"If I need it. I think so. I've never tried it on another human."

The hail calmed, and lazy flurries wafted down, visible from the window and backlit by the porch light. Hunter collected himself and looked back at the beauty that stood before him, cradling her plant as if it were a baby, warmth from his fireplace curling around her like a comforting embrace, her hair drying with a frizz he had not yet seen on her.

Adorable.

"I love this," Olivia said, pressing her fingers up from the bottom of the plant with a delighted sigh.

"Wait until we dig into those Danishes, if houseplants alone cause that serene look on your face," Hunter said.

"It's peaceful. The way the soil feels. It's *alive*. More alive than you, than me." She knelt down to place the poinsettia into the pot and scooped the dirt around it. She then brought up another handful, marveling at the way it crumbled between her fingers. "I can feel it breathing. The roots whisper when you touch them. I almost never get to touch roots like this."

Hunter listened but frowned. "I don't hear them whispering."

"That's because you don't listen," she teased, flashing him a bright smile. He was getting used to that now, her smiling. He had guessed, in true goth fashion, that she would bloom only doom and gloom when he first led her out of that forest. Instead, it was starting to feel like Christmas.

Christmas.

It hadn't felt like Christmas since Sarah was here.

Yet here Olivia was, and she accomplished it without even trying, just by being herself, unapologetically. Hunter was still scared shitless of her, as he should be, but he didn't regret it; he didn't regret bringing her here.

That cop may have regretted it.

Hunter's lips quirked, but he wasn't convinced he'd done a good enough job easing the sadness and worry that continued to creep into his head and heart. "So, what are the roots telling you?"

Olivia looked into his eyes, and he knew she saw, saw that he was damaged and hurt. Healing wasn't impossible, but it was a damn journey. She didn't say anything, though, as if that were her way of saying she understood, as if that were her way of saying, "Me too." Instead, she closed her eyes and rolled her shoulders back, cracking her neck as she tilted her ear to her shoulder on both sides. "That you're terrible at potting plants."

Hunter barked out a laugh. He couldn't help it. "That's slander. I poured the dirt like a professional."

Olivia looked back down to inspect their work. The bright red leaves were disheveled and looked worse for wear. They were either resistant to the new home they had been gifted or to being out of Olivia's arms, her hands prodding at their roots.

I understand.

Hunter was commiserating with plants now.

"We should put a second one in it. You didn't buy enough planters for one per pot."

"I'm sure some of them can be gentlemen and sleep on the couch."

Olivia raised her eyebrows, not understanding the joke.

It was a bad joke. Of course, she didn't understand it.

Hunter made a mental note to see if he could find jokes from the early 1900s. He liked seeing her laugh, so maybe he could make her laugh on purpose.

"Two per pot," she confirmed, moving back to the coffee table and gently pulling another poinsettia from its plastic wrapping. She brought it back to the window, to him, to the planter pot. She set it, her eyes evoking love and pride, a chemist celebrating the first explosive they made in their humble home garage lab.

"You really can't hear them?" she asked.

He couldn't.

Of course, he couldn't. It was absurd. It was a joke. He indulged it for her because, for her, it was real. She had magic, a connection to something he had taken for granted his entire life. He hadn't deserved to hear them. He would be ashamed to listen to what they had to say if he could.

Hunter was sure of it.

14

CHAPTER FOURTEEN.

Hunter and Olivia worked, finishing the job together as she hummed. He tried not to stare at her with lovesick puppy eyes. His brain worked hard to push him away from her again, and he began to let it. It had become a maddening cycle—his heart swinging between fire and ice, forever undone by his wild, secretive tree siren.

You belong to her.

His hands gripped the bag of dirt as he filled the last planter pot, then lugged it into the kitchen. He set the pot in front of the door that led to the backyard.

But do you? Maybe she regrets it, coming here with you, with someone who can't hear the sounds of the forest, the secrets of trees, the passion of the growing—the living—plants and botanicals that she covets.

"The light is wonderful." Olivia didn't have to work hard to convince him. Her eyelashes did that all on their own—he folded under that mysterious, seductive, heart-touching stare, hoping that there was no murderous intent running through her mind in case he told her no.

Maybe you like it, the danger of her. Maybe you need it.

"We might need to be able to open the door," he sighed, a headache sneaking in, mixed with the too little and unrestful slumber that he got from the couch, catching up to him.

Don't let her regret it.

The last of the poinsettias stood tall and proud, nearly pining over Olivia's touch, leaves stretching out as her soft hands pulled away. Hunter imagined that if he could hear them like she was so sure that she could, he would hear them whimpering, begging, worshipping the woman who put her soul into their care.

Hunter walked over to the kitchen counter, where the still slightly wet Danish box sat, forgotten about until now. He lifted the lid and grabbed the one with candied oranges, taking a large bite, cream and jelly oozing into his mouth. His stomach let out a large gargle in response, and Hunter smiled, the sugar making him instantly happy.

He turned to Olivia, who stood frozen in place, watching him eat. She still wore the same black sweater dress his mom had chosen for her. It clung from the dampness of rain and their kisses, now dry but streaked with dirt from working so close to the mantle and the fire. The flames crackled in the living room after he'd poked them and added another log.

"Here, let me get you one," Hunter said, opening the cupboard and bringing down a plate, only to drop it, startled by Olivia's ability to appear right next to him without making a sound.

The ceramic cracked at his feet.

"Shit," he said, jumping back. "Are you okay? I'm so sorry."

You're blowing it, man.

He couldn't tell if Olivia was hurt. If she were, she didn't say. Instead, her warm breath exhaled, her lips aimed up at him as she closed her eyes and opened her mouth.

"I'll try a bite."

Hunter pulled a piece of the dough off his own Danish and

carefully popped it into Olivia's mouth. He could feel her heat, her fire on his thumb and forefinger.

What would it feel like if she closed those lips around my fingers?

She didn't, only closing her mouth after she pulled away, while he watched a twitch appear in her cheek. Her eyes opened, and a magical sparkle suddenly appeared, an almost childlike joy as her eyes moistened.

"It tastes like Christmas," she said, before backing up and turning away from him, bending down to the pots, petting the poinsettia leaves.

"What's wrong?" Hunter asked, worry filling him as he saw the slump in her shoulders, the slight hanging of her head, the sudden silence that hadn't existed between them even once that day.

Instead of answering, she swooped back around, tossing her frizzy hair that somehow made her more beautiful, more of what he would have guessed a forest goddess would look like. It was as if she had been drawn, a character version of herself that only existed in the minds of people who were far more talented than him.

She is real. Sarah, she is real. This is real.

Olivia was back at his side, her mouth open again, waiting for Hunter's offering of more Danish. She wasn't going to tell him, whatever it was. She didn't trust him with whatever that was, at least not yet.

"I'm here for you," he promised, offering her another bite of the Danish. She chewed slowly, a look of relief softening her features, as if the sugar flooding her veins for the first time in far too long brought her back to life. When her eyes opened again, they held something different—something new.

"More," she demanded, the softness in her tone gone, replaced only by demand, need, and want.

Hunter would not refuse her and instead picked up a new Danish from the box, holding it up to her mouth. She opened her mouth, taking half the Danish into her mouth before biting down on the blue and red berries with powdered sugar. Hunter's cock stiffened, and he forced himself to swallow, his eyes flicking to the ceiling out of respect.

If she doesn't trust me, I can change that. I can earn it.

But it wasn't trust she needed—not right then.

Maybe she just wanted to hide.

Or maybe she wanted to be there with him.

She placed her hand on his wrist and raised his hand to his own mouth as he took a bite.

"More," she said through those eyelashes.

Fuck me.

He obliged. "It's the last one."

"You eat," she said. Hunter opened his mouth, and as he did, Olivia grabbed his shirt and pulled his face down to hers as she bit the other end of the Danish. Sweetness exploded in Hunter's mouth, crumbled flaky dough falling between them, white cream filling dribbling down Olivia's chin as she still held his shirt down, as she did not indicate that she would let go.

Olivia chewed and swallowed, licking her lips, and extending her neck up to Hunter's, her eyes staring into his. His whole body relaxed, wanting to fall into her, this odd comfort, this warmth that he found in the little woman with a magical voice. She seemed to know what she wanted; and maybe what she wanted was him.

She kissed you. You kissed her back.

And he was all hers, even though he wouldn't be wrong to question his sanity or if he should run, if he should have taken her to the police station and said he found this missing person. If his mom did truly join a church, there had to be some kind of program to set Olivia up with so she wouldn't be alone.

No, she wouldn't be alone because you wouldn't let her be.

Hunter pulled back, panting. "Olivia." Even her name on

his lips sent his body into a spiral—tense, needy, wondering what other parts of her body smelled like, tasted like.

But Olivia wasn't accepting his words, his hesitation, and instead brought her mouth to his again, silencing him. Their lips danced once more, and her hips moved forward into his while her hands found their way into his hair, massaging his scalp and the back of his neck.

She let him out of his willing hostage situation and looked down at the bulge in his pants, smiling proudly at her work.

"You've never had a man." He raised an eyebrow at his question.

"That is something that seems easy to change," she said, and let her head roll back around, her hair swaying off of her shoulders as her hips grinded against him, presenting her chest, her neck to him.

Control, Hunter. Have fucking control.

If Sarah couldn't be here, if he went feral for a woman for the first time since she had passed away, he would do it right, he would do it honorably. This was not a rebound. Olivia would not be an outlet for his grief.

Hunter grabbed her hips and kissed up her jawline tenderly, bringing the escalation of their heat back down to a gentle simmer. She moaned, the softest little sound that made him, for the first time, want to bite into someone's throat, claim them for him and only him.

How could he stop this? How could he tell her, with words too clumsy for a creature like her, that she was the most achingly beautiful thing he had ever seen—that even the moon must envy the way she pulled the tides of his heart?

How could he confess that every glance, every soft sigh, carved him open—only to ask her to wait?

Because he did want her.

God, he needed her.

But not like this.

Not hurried and breathless on a kitchen counter, not tangled in potting soil and powdered sugar, not while the cold dirt of the world still clung to them both.

Their first time, her first time, should be worship. A moment that would haunt him long after the last leaf fell from the trees. She had been his for less than a day, yet already he knew: if she turned her back and melted into the forest shadows once more, he would follow her into that darkness without a single heartbeat of doubt. He would surrender everything just to find her there again.

"Olivia," he gasped again, her hands moving down his chest, lower and lower, dangerously close to the bulge that made her proud, that told her what a good little tree siren she was, that made him want to show her exactly how proud she should be.

Knock. Knock. Knock.

Thank God.

"Come back," Olivia pouted. Her face slightly scared him, her protruding lip more a threat than something cute and playful.

"Someone's at the door, and they don't usually go away."

Knock. Knock. Knock.

"See?"

Olivia sighed. "Do you usually have so many visitors?"

"Unfortunately, yes, no one can ever seem to just leave me alone."

Knock. Knock. Knock.

"Hunter, I know you're in there," he could hear through the door, recognizing the voice.

Olivia raised her eyebrows.

"See, they never can just go away," he shrugged, moving out of the kitchen but taking her hand in his, not leaving her alone, not showing any indication that he was rejecting her. It was the opposite; he wanted her by his side. The world should know, the world should meet Olivia.

"I'm coming, hang on," Hunter yelled, approaching the front door, gently pulling Olivia behind him. The lock unclicked, and the natural light framed Sadie standing there, hip popped out and arms crossed. She looked at him from underneath her glasses.

"You look like shit," she snorted.

"Ah, yeah, we were potting some plants."

"We?"

Hunter moved to the side so Olivia was more visible, and Sadie's eyes widened in disbelief.

"You—you have another friend? When did this happen? I thought you were sick."

"Oh, Sadie, you'll always be my best pal." Hunter laughed. "Who knew you were so possessive?"

"I'm too old to be recruiting new friends every time my usual speed dial grows up and moves on. Hi, I'm Sadie."

Olivia stared back, not replying, not smiling. Hunter's gaze moved back and forth between the two until he couldn't take the silence any longer.

"Now that that's out of the way, I really was sick."

He wasn't lying. The first few times he had heard Olivia sing had so drastically altered his mind that he could not be responsible for his actions, for his memory. People stayed home these days with common colds, and this seemed much worse than that.

"Well, I just came to check on you." Sadie cleared her throat. "Don't invite me in or anything—it's freezing outside."

"I'm afraid to invite you in to be honest," Hunter admitted. "There's potting soil everywhere. Turns out I can't pour dirt out of a bag without bits spraying all over the room."

Sadie laughed. "Is this another one of your vinegar experiments?"

You really have to stop telling people about your hobbies.

"I can still smell it, by the way. But at least it's not knocking me out this time. I approve." She held out an off-white, sparkly envelope. "Your big prize from the raffle. Tickets to the Christmas Eve ball. I'm sure you're just dying to waltz back into your old wedding venue. What could possibly go wrong?"

Hunter took them as the phone in his pocket vibrated a few times. Sadie mirrored him, pulling out her own. Chimes rang over and over and over again between the two devices.

"Group chat." Hunter shook his head. "I said no more group chats."

As if a group of coworkers would listen to him.

CELIA 2:53 PM:

Winter break biatches. Reminder that we are doing a meetup at the downtown holiday market tomorrow, 6pm sharp.

NINA 2:53 PM:

Does anyone remember if it's cash only?

DARIUS 2:54 PM:

Who's going to be my ride buddy?

ELAINE 2:55PM:

There are like two rides and they are for children.

NINA 2:55 PM:

Woah, woah, children don't get dibs on everything fun.

DARIUS 2:55 PM:

As long as there's a good pilsner, I'll be there.

Sadie's fingers began typing, a playful smile sneaking onto her face.

SADIE 2:55 PM:

Can we bring a plus one?

ELAINE 2:56 PM:

"Sadie, who are you bringing?"

SADIE 2:56 PM:

"I'm not asking for me."

Her chin was raised towards Olivia as she said to Hunter, "I'm talking about your charming new friend here. Lovely conversationalist, she is."

Hunter shook his head.

HUNTER 2:56 PM:

"Can we skip the black cat energy?"

NINA 2:57 PM:

I'm bringing Tom.

DARIUS 2:57 PM:

Who's Tom?

NINA 2:57 PM:

My husband, who you've met nineteen times.

DARIUS 2:58 PM:

His name is Tom and you expect me to remember him?

SADIE 2:58 PM:

Hunter is bringing his new lady friend.

NINA 2:58 PM:

HUNTER DOES NOT HAVE A NEW LADY
FRIEND.

SADIE 2:58 PM:

Oh, he does. I'm looking at her right now. He
looks like he might kill me.

DARIUS 2:59 PM:

Atta boy, hound dog.

HUNTER 2:59 PM:

Do not call me a hound dog.

DARIUS 2:59 PM:

I think it's going to stick.

"Sadie, what the hell?" Hunter growled at her.

Olivia reached out her hand protectively in front of Hunter's chest, like she was planning on attacking, on defending something that was hers.

"This feels hostile now." Sadie took a step away, Olivia's eyes going dark, almost vacant. The hairs on the back of Hunter's arms stood up, a chill running down his spine.

Hunter gulped, worry flooding his heart, his chest as he looked over to Olivia, praying that what his eyes conveyed was not nefarious, that Sadie would not be lying on his porch dead in the next few breaths.

"Thanks for these," Hunter said, holding up the envelope. "You're a good friend, Sadie."

"You mean the best," Sadie said, slugging his shoulder but

shooting a nervous glance at Olivia. "I'll leave you two crazy kids to it. I'll see you tomorrow. Both of you then?"

Hunter had no doubt that she regretted roping Olivia into this, and he would panic and deal with the implications of dragging his little tree siren out into the world.

"We will be there," he said.

"This was plenty awkward," Sadie said, turning around, hands in her jacket pockets as she walked off toward her car parked on the curb.

15

CHAPTER FIFTEEN.

"Who is this?" Olivia demanded the next morning.

Something sharp poked his chin, so Hunter forced his eyes open, his body sore from another night on the couch. A lone bird was chirping as the light flooded the house. It was early, far too early.

Olivia stood over him, wearing his oversized clothes again, with a framed photo in her hand. It was another photo of Sarah, in her wedding dress, arm in arm with Hunter, carrying a bouquet of red roses. They were both smiling, happy, in love, and safe.

"Where did you find that?" he asked, sitting up, taking it from her, and running his fingers over Sarah's face. It was the opposite of Olivia's; there was no mystery there, no hollowness, only proof of a thriving life. She had brought so much of that life to him.

"It was behind some boxes in the back of your closet. Is that her? Your wife?"

Hunter looked up into Olivia's face. There was an eagerness

there for this discussion. Although he wasn't entirely ready, he might as well try.

"She died three years ago this coming May," he said. "She was a scientist working with food preservatives. The chemical she worked with sucked all the oxygen out of the room, and three others died with her."

Hunter let himself live in the silence that grew between them, the both of them processing a life he'd lived that Olivia would never know.

"She was the love of my life, Olivia. I never could express the pain that I have been dealing with. It's as if my heart had gone missing. I loved her. I loved her more than I've loved anything, anyone. When she died, I died too."

Olivia nodded. "When I was young, I hoped to marry a man who could speak so romantically. To be his sun."

Hunter smiled softly and took the frame out of Olivia's hands, setting it beside him on the couch. "You are no sun, Olivia."

She frowned, chin down. His words had hurt her. She started to pull away.

"Let me finish," he said, his gentle grip tightening, finding bravery in their new, fragile relationship. "You are the moon, you are the stars, a candle aflame. The only light is when darkness wraps itself around you. You are a cool breeze on my face, reminding me that I am here and alive and can keep living."

Olivia's hands went limp in his. She raised her chin, her eyes gleaming from held-back tears.

"I'm sorry, Olivia, I'm broken. But I am trying to heal. I really am trying. Maybe it's all for you."

"I'm broken, too," she said. "And maybe your words, your song can mend me."

"My song?"

"Thank you," she said before grabbing the frame from the

couch. "I can go put this back. It just seemed so hidden, so lonely. It made me sad for her."

"Like I was sad to hear that you hid away in a tree."

Olivia nodded.

Hunter stood. "How about I make some coffee? We've got a big night tonight. Are you sure you want to go? You don't have to. My colleagues' peer pressure isn't serious."

"I'll go," she said with a sad smile. "I've never been to a holiday market before."

"I'll see if we can get you some more clothes," he said, walking over to the kitchen, swiping his phone off the counter, and texting his mom. Before he could grab the kettle off the gas stove, his phone dinged, a reply back on his unlocked home screen.

MOM 6:33 AM:

I WOULD LOVE TO.

The oven squeaked as Hunter opened it. Decorative oven mitts covered his hands, and he pulled out a hot sheet pan with the only gourmet single-guy meal he had the ingredients stocked to make.

Olivia had been zipping around the house, humming to the poinsettias and mistletoe, making them all grow before Hunter's eyes, their colors and brilliance illuminating like expensive fake house plants he remembered seeing at open houses.

Hunter watched as Olivia kissed their petals, and he couldn't tell if he was imagining it, but he thought he could hear them coo back to her, babies cheering in delight as the rolls under their chins were tickled. She was quirky, and he liked it; he liked it so much.

"What are these?" Olivia skipped into the kitchen, a stack of thick gilded cards in her hands, vivid with silver and mystical etchings.

"Those were one of Sarah's newer hobbies—tarot cards. They are supposed to tell you about the future, the past. I've tried to learn, too, but didn't get very far."

"What is that then?" Olivia followed as Hunter threw the hot pan down on the stovetop.

"Tortilla chips with melted cheese," Hunter said. "This breakfast has gotten me through many hard days."

"Is today going to be a hard day?"

Hunter turned, her face inches away from his, and realised he was already so comfortable with her. He was getting more used to her forwardness, her assertiveness, her possession of him, of sorts. It was a very different type of belonging than how he held onto her, a silent worship that existed from more of a distance. Hunter preferred to watch, to observe, to feel safe.

Safe was the opposite of Olivia.

"What do your cards tell you about me, Hunter?" Olivia asked, holding out the deck to him. He took it and looked down at the drawing of a woman with her head up towards the sky.

He didn't know what it meant. He hadn't a clue.

"Your magic, your power, whatever you call it, did your parents have it too?" he asked.

Olivia shook her head no. "I watched my mother grow sad and cold as she tried her best to help me cover it up. No one knew where it came from."

"Are there others like you?" Hunter sloppily shuffled the cards in his hand.

"I don't know. I've been alone my entire life in this."

"I'm sorry," Hunter said. She must have been so lonely.

"What would you ask the cards if I knew how to read them better?"

Olivia paused, considering. "I would ask them if you are the right one. If you are who I am looking for."

Hunter held his breath. She was so forward that he didn't

have enough time to explore his own heart before he could decide. His consciousness filled with light and dark, pulling him like a rope in a tug of war. The dark often won; Olivia often won over his voice of reason.

"What if I am?"

"Then you better be sure, Hunter. Because I will never let go once you tell me not to."

Did he want that?

He couldn't be sure what was real, what was haze, what was spell. If he told her no, would this all just disappear? Could he even go back to what his pathetic life was before he met a maiden in a forest, before he offered to be a shining white knight, before the universe laughed at his intentions?

Hunter set the cards on a pile of papers and junk on the back countertop as Olivia walked up to the pan and sniffed, taking a chip and watching as the cheese pulled, long and stringy. She frowned, put it back and turned to walk away, back to singing to the poinsettia, back to exploring every drawer that he had in this house.

He grabbed her hand, stopping her, and she snapped into him, her body so close, her warmth radiating onto him.

"Today will be a lot. I don't blame you if you change your mind or'd rather not go. I can stay here with you, too. Honestly, I would be perfectly content to watch a movie with you, maybe talk a little."

"A movie?" Olivia frowned.

"Moving pictures. They tell a story, remember? On the TV?"

Olivia crossed her arms over her chest. "You were supposed to get rid of it. The tree, it's too uncomfortable; it's crying out for help. I thought you, Hunter, would understand and take action."

Hunter rolled his eyes.

"Silly me for wanting to spend some time with you, for thinking I could have you all to myself."

"This isn't about me," Olivia scoffed. "This is about the tree. And how dare you hold me to blame for your feelings of insecurity?"

Hunter watched her stomp out of the kitchen.

Insecurity? How am I insecure?

"Why are you mad, Olivia?"

Get real. She's right. You're incredibly insecure about yourself, about her, about what Sarah might think.

"Because I'll have to sing to make you listen to me, but then you won't really be there. Not in the way I need you. I thought you could be someone real in my life, someone I can count on, like the roots under the ground. Not someone I would have to control."

Hunter felt his heart skip a beat, fear inching its way back in as he stared at the sweet, sad, and fallen face of a real monster, an enchantress whom he treated as someone kind, someone loving, and gentle.

My tree siren.

It was a cute pet name for his inner monologue, but perhaps it covered up the very real threat that she did possess, that she could hold over his head: that she held his free will in the palm of her hands.

She needed to go back to the forest.

"You would do that? Even now?" Hunter asked, his voice barely more than a whisper. She heard him, though, judging by the way her body tightened and how her shoulders pulled closer together. Olivia stood, keeping her back towards him until, after a few breaths, her head fell, a show of defeat.

Hunter, so filled with adrenaline that he kept inside, that he felt obligated to hide from view, reached his hand out for her shoulder, but then let it fall.

She will control you, strip you of your autonomy. *That cannot turn into a relationship, so what are you doing here with her?*

This was an dishonor to Sarah. The idea that this could have been anything more than a rebound was a joke.

"I would," Olivia admitted. "I will protect myself, Hunter. Just like I've always had to."

Pain—she carried so much pain. That, Hunter could understand. That, he related to. Her grief, her despair, knowing that who you once were could never exist again, so you then begin to mourn yourself, your smiles, your laughs, your genuine hope and excitement for a future that would never exist.

Fuck it.

His steps were quick and wide as he moved past Olivia into the hallway and turned into his room. After digging under the bed, he pulled out a golf club laced with dust that had once been gifted to him by someone who wrongly thought he'd enjoy the sport. He kept it because he thought it could be a useful weapon for a break-in; he didn't have the guts to keep a gun in his room.

Hunter stomped back towards the living room, hands gripping the black rubbery top of the club. Olivia watched him, her nose crinkled in a way that was too damn cute, so he quickly looked away from her so he wouldn't lose his focus, his nerve.

"What's going to happen?" Olivia's ethereal voice sounded too close to the song, as if she were warming her vocal chords.

"Don't sing. Not yet." Hunter demanded.

"Why?"

"I'll show you why." With tremendous force, Hunter took his left hand and pushed the television off the shelf. Olivia jumped back with a scream, but a wicked smile danced across her lips. The dark, solemn glaze that had sunken over her eyes lifted as Hunter experimented, as he gave her what she asked for: someone who listened.

Hunter let the golf club fall beside him as he grabbed the thirty-inch television and pulled it so forcefully that the cord was yanked out of the socket, snapping as the metal prongs bent backwards. He threw the screen down onto the floor. Olivia yelped again at the bang and then giggled, clapping her hands before her chin.

Hunter reached down, clasping the thin metal golf club between his hands, and raised it over his head, hitting the ceiling and sending mistletoe and white drywall crumbling down over them, as if encasing them in a real-life snowglobe.

"This is for the tree," Hunter yelled as he brought the club down. The thick head broke the screen, creating a web with fat shards waiting to be freed and released.

"Yes," Olivia screamed.

Hunter raised the club again.

"This is for you," he said, bringing it back down.

"Yes!" Olivia jumped, her smile beaming.

Once more, Hunter raised his club, feeling liberated, like he could do no wrong, that he could be destructive, that he could show the world his hurt for the first time, that he could show the way that he wanted to heal.

He wanted to heal with her, with his tree siren.

"This is for me." He smashed the television screen with one more forceful swing down, this one loudest of all, as wires poked through, and a hole four inches wide now existed where there once was a working television.

Break it all. Light the house on fire.

Hunter breathed slowly, in through his nose, out from his mouth as the anger that was hidden beneath his skin writhed, an awakened beast, testosterone running through his veins as his body urged him to keep breaking more shit. To erase it all, all of the memories that kept him stuck here, stuck here with Sarah.

Why can't I let go?

With Olivia watching him, Hunter knew it was now or never. It was time to choose. He couldn't continue living this way, even if Olivia disappeared, even if he had woken up and realized that this was all some wicked, terrible, heartbreaking dream. He needed to move forward, and though that didn't mean leaving Sarah behind, it meant making real space, a real effort to bring more into his life.

Knock. Knock. Knock.

Worst possible timing.

Hunter dropped the club, staring into Olivia's mischievous eyes. His hand twitched, and he opened his mouth wide, popping his jaw, a wildness still pushing his heart rate up.

With heavy footsteps, he stalked towards the door, his neck turning, arching as he refused to give up his eye contact with the woman who brought something new out of him, the woman that made him unleash a new man within himself, one that had been dormant, one that he was surprised had ever existed.

His body was rigid, his hands balled into fists, a peacock showing off its feathers as Olivia stared right back.

Is that pride in her eyes?

She was proud of him. She was proud of how feral he could become. How feral he was for her. If it weren't for that knock at the door, he might have had to reconsider their first time being right, being romantic. This was the most goddamn romantic thing he had done for anyone.

Hunter gritted his teeth and pulled the door handle back. He was pent up, uncontrollably irritated that he had again been interrupted, and he feared for whoever was there, needing to be in his space. Someone always had to be in his space.

He was a goddamn grown man. And he was okay.

He just liked pickles.

At least I have hobbies. I could be a loser.

When the cold intruded on the space, sneaking in like a welcomed pest as the door hung wide open, Hunter saw nothing.

There's no one here.

His jaw tightened, rage simmering hotter with every second. Being interrupted for a foolish reason was bad enough. Being interrupted for no reason at all was something else entirely. He stepped out onto the porch, scanning the street for a car creeping away, but instead felt a crisp crunch beneath his boot. Bracing himself against the doorframe, Hunter glanced down. Three retail shopping bags, thick paper, garishly bright, each flaunting a different store's logo, sat brimming at his feet.

Mom.

He'd asked his mom to drop off clothes. He didn't realize that she would go shopping for an entirely new wardrobe.

Generous. She was always too generous.

Hunter couldn't stand it. He wished he knew why it bothered him so much to have so much support. Really, what he craved, what he wanted, was no support at all. To be left out in the middle of the woods, with only a knife in hand and a wound on his cheek.

Olivia was teaching him that, teaching him who he could be. His eyes opened for the first time, and he was a newborn, fresh and ready for a world that would try to eat him alive.

But together, they could stop that. Together, the world couldn't touch either of them.

Hunter grabbed the bags and slammed the door, locking it.

"These are for you," he muttered. "My mom must really like you. I don't think she ever bought Sarah an entire rack from a department store."

"Hunter," Olivia said, her voice vacant and eerie despite the devastatingly sweet smile on her face. "We need to bury it."

"Bury it?"

She motioned towards the television. "It still vibrates, hums. If you prefer to keep smashing, you can. It just won't be enough."

"Enough?" Hunter swallowed. "All of this wasn't enough?"

Olivia let out an exhale, showing obvious disappointment

in his reaction. She shook her head as her eyes darkened to onyx black as she opened her mouth and cleared her throat.

"For the tree, there can never be enough."

Olivia sang.

"Sweet Silver Bells

Throw Cares Away."

On the first line, Hunter's mind went hazy. On the second,he realized whatever immunity he'd thought he had was a severe mistake as his vision went black.

16

CHAPTER SIXTEEN.

Pain tore through Hunter the moment he drifted back to consciousness, his world no wider than the darkness behind his eyelids. His knuckles throbbed, each fingertip a raw nerve set ablaze. He scraped his index finger across his thumbnail and nearly screamed, but his lips refused to part, split and frozen, the skin on his face searing as if he had stood too long against a merciless wind, frost biting deep into his cheeks and brow.

There was nothing there at all—no nail on his thumb, the flesh underneath excruciating to the touch.

What happened?

He racked his brain, twitching various parts of his body, checking to see what else was injured. He calmed after he'd finished his inspection, learning that he was mostly sore and that the most serious damage was in his hands, his missing nail, and his knuckles.

His eyelids fluttered open, and he found himself back on the couch. It wasn't morning this time, and he was still dressed in the same clothes as before. The smell of dirt clung to him, but it lacked the soft sweetness of potting soil. This was rancid, ancient, the stench of decay and old earth, as if he had crawled through tunnels burrowed too close to leaking pipes and something foul that festered and fed on anything alive.

The haze still lingered, creeping through his thoughts, blurring the edges of what came before. The last thing he could grasp were those dark eyes—unyielding, merciless, carved from a hunger that would not be denied. She would take what she wanted. She would claim what she needed.

"Olivia," he croaked, trying to roll on his side. He heard no noise, no response.

Where is she?

Hunter's heart plummeted to the pit of his stomach.

Is she gone?

And if so, did she leave or was she taken?

If the cops had suspected her, had figured out that she was here, looking for the officer's murderer, surely he would be aware.

You're a fool. No one could take Olivia against her will.

Of course not. If someone tried, he did not doubt that there would be more bodies to add to the collection of the dead, those who were victims of Olivia's voice.

Her voice.

She had sung to him, and the haze was beginning to lift. She'd used him. She'd told him that he wasn't enough, and she'd used him.

For what, he didn't know, but his missing fingernails were more than enough proof that he had not been lying on the couch to rest.

Hunter wasn't sure if he was worried, scared, or angry, so he settled at the point where all three of those emotions met.

"Olivia," he yelled, and winced when the back of his hand and his fingertips rubbed against the back of the sofa.

Silence.

Fuck.

Hunter took a deep breath and held it in, as if he were about to dive underwater. He marched right out the front door, leaving it open behind him. The air stung against his raw face, while light snowflakes and small amounts of rain hit and sizzled on his lips. He looked over towards the tree, where Olivia sat on the ground.

Her face was in her hands, and she was hunched over, sobbing, wearing clothes that undoubtedly came from the collection his mom had gone out and shopped for. Most of the front lawn was covered in snow, but the six feet around Olivia had obviously been disturbed. Ground and dirt flailed around her, dirtying and graying the lawn.

The area before her looked like a grave. A freshly dug grave.

Hunter looked down at his hands again, the skin raw, a fingernail gone, his knuckles aching.

No. No, that can't be it.

"Olivia," he uttered, too afraid to ask. He supposed that was what bravery was, though—doing something even when you were terrified, even when you expected the worst possible outcome.

There had to be another cop. Why else would she be sobbing in front of a freshly dug grave?

Olivia's shoulders tightened, and she sat up, looking down at the recently moved earth, not daring to meet his eyes.

"Please tell me what happened."

She shook her head. "I can't."

He walked toward her, boots still on his feet that did not press into the slush or snow because of the dirt stuck in the tread pattern.

"Olivia, you can tell me anything," he said, his steps stopping when she turned her head, her eyes meeting his. He might have stopped because of that fear, but what it really was was heartbreak evident across her beautiful face.

His girl. His moon. His tree siren.

Hunter couldn't watch her cry. He realized that he would kill all the police if it meant never again having to see her cry. For the first time in his life, he made a mental note to buy a hatchet. If he went down for Olivia, it would be swinging.

"Hey, hey." Feelings that had frozen him now had him moving, rushing toward her and blanketing her in his arms, not minding the bite of the exposed skin on his fingers. "I've got you. I'm here. I'll always be here. Olivia, I'm not going anywhere."

She rested her head on his shoulder as they sat beside the grave, her sobs spilling out in shivers against his coat. Hunter noticed every car that crawled past, felt his pulse jump whenever a horn blared or a stranger with a leashed dog paused to ask if they were alright. He was used to it by now—being the hushed topic behind closed doors ever since Sarah's death, the neighbor everyone watched from behind curtains. He could live with the stares, the whispers. So he pulled her closer, pressed his face into the curve of her neck, and breathed her in.

What a spectacle we are.

The world outside was lucky to take it in.

Hunter raised his face to Olivia's, wiping a tear off of her beautiful, smooth skin, blinded by the horror that was his hands. She didn't seem to mind or notice; she only looked at him.

"The grave, did I dig it?" he asked.

"Yes." Her voice was bursting out, pushed forward by her sobs.

"We couldn't find a shovel?"

"It doesn't work that way."

"What do you mean?"

Olivia got up to her feet, snow crunching underneath her. "I just say what's in my heart, and it's done, my song and wishes moving through someone's brain. The order is obtuse, general; I don't control any specifics. You chose to dig by hand."

"I didn't choose anything." Hunter rose to match her. She looked at her feet, her head hanging in shame.

"That's why I'm crying," she whispered. "I'm so sorry. I didn't want to control you. Something takes over me, my heart sings out and then suddenly, I'm a monster, a witch, the most horrifying of nightmares."

Hunter's mouth gaped open.

She's ashamed.

"What?" She took a step back. "What does the expression on your face mean?"

Hunter shook his head and ran his hand through his hair, wincing, forgetting about his missing fingernails.

"Everything you say, whenever you open those beautiful lips, I somehow fall even harder for you."

Olivia let out a cry, burying her face in her hands again. "You're not angry? You're not sending me away?"

Hunter shook his head and brought Olivia into his chest, his arms wrapped around her tightly. "I don't think I could send you away."

Olivia sniffed, "You're right. I wouldn't let you."

Though it was a very real threat, Hunter reveled in it. He somehow needed her, and she seemed to need him. It was that simple, their differences aside.

"Who did I bury, Olivia?"

Her body shuddered under his weight until he could feel her back expanding and contracting, her breath steadying as she gathered the nerve to say.

Ages, multiple lives where their souls still connected, must have passed by as Hunter waited, until Olivia had finally found it, that courage. Hunter's eyes widened, his body began to tremble when the words came out of her mouth, finalizing it, knowing that it could never be repaired.

"The television."

Laughter erupted from him. He couldn't remember the last time he had laughed like that, felt joy and relief in a way where he felt ten years younger, where he could go through the darkest depths of hell with a smile, knowing that this happiness, this purest, most innocent sensation pulsed through him.

He was smiling like an idiot as he marveled at her confusion.

"I dug a grave with my bare hands in the snow, in the frozen dirt, for my television?"

Olivia nodded, her face solemn, untrusting of Hunter's grace.

"Is the tree happier at least?"

She considered, looking at the bare-branched dark tree hovering too close to his roof, promising a gutter filled with leaves this next fall.

"It certainly appreciates it," she said. "But I expect you'll have a long way to go before happiness is its reality."

"Will you help me get there?"

This made her smile. He would talk about trees all day if that were what stopped the tears.

"I will."

Hunter's phone chimed. Then it chimed again. And again.

I hate group texts.

He pulled it out of his back pocket, impressed that it hadn't somehow been buried with the television since it rarely could stay in his pocket, and stared at the unlocked screen.

CELIA 4: 54 PM:

See you all in an hour.

DARIUS 4:55 PM:

Do I still have to meet Tom?

NINA 4:56 PM:

You've met Tom so many times.

SADIE 4:57 PM:

RIP Tom.

NINA: 4:57 PM:

NOT FUNNY!

ELAINE 4:58 PM:

Calm down, Nina.

"I've got to get inside and shower for the holiday market," Hunter said, wrapping his arm around Olivia's waist and moving her inside with him.

17

CHAPTER SEVENTEEN.

"There are so many lights," Olivia said disapprovingly as Hunter circled around eight times, trying to find a parking spot.

"It's a big decoration for the holidays," he said, sliding into a tight spot, knowing he'd have to do some weird things with his hips to get his body out of the car.

"Did they even think to ask the trees?"

"You didn't put lights everywhere when you celebrated?"

Olivia shook her head. "Garlands, yes, and candles were lit but generally not around greenery that would quickly kindle flame unless they were safe in a lantern."

"Unfortunately, I don't think many people are considering whether the trees are okay with the Christmas lights."

Olivia crossed her arms over her chest.

"Look, we don't have to be here. You look incredible in these new clothes, but much as I'd love to show you off, I'd love to stay in our small bubble, our secret little world, for so much longer than we have."

Her arms uncrossed as her hand reached out and was placed on his neck. His heartbeat rose as she moved her face close to his, the fading twilight engulfing them in intimacy that he'd never predicted he would experience again.

"Our little bubble," she let the words coat her tongue like luxurious champagne. "I love the way that sounds."

He could feel her warm breath on his skin. Her teasing lips were just inches from his. He wanted to push forward, close their gap, but he waited. He rooted himself in self-control and lounged in the lusciousness of her essence until she spoke again.

"Let's not disappoint your friends, Hunter. This is how I repay your kindness. I will participate in your life, add to it, and be a part of it."

That wasn't his love language. If anything, he would rather be around people less. He preferred less caring, less effort. That bubble would pop, and who knew if they could ever rebuild it. Who knew what could happen when others got involved in their relationship when it was so new?

"I'm always happy with just us, so you know," he told her, his hand on her cheek. She bit her lip.

That damn beautiful bottom lip.

"Let's go," he sighed, realizing that no, she wouldn't change her mind and they would likely spend the night discussing how angry the trees were. The teacher's lounge after the break would surely be quiet when he walked into it since no one would know how to handle someone like Olivia, no one would understand why he held onto her so fast and so tight. He didn't want to explain it to anyone.

They stepped out of the car into a winter wonderland, all of Market Street closed and blocked off, transformed in twenty-four hours. Tents and pop-up booths lined the sidewalks, all adorned with hanging lights and sparkling artificial snowflakes.

The air had a tinge of holiday magic, the cold kissing Hunter's cheeks in welcome as he walked under hundreds of feet of green garland hanging with bright red ribbons between vintage copper light posts.

Olivia walked beside him, her gloved hand intertwined with his. He tried not to wince from the soreness of his missing thumbnail.

It's nothing you can't deal with.

Olivia looked so normal. She was beautifully, heartbreakingly normal. She wasn't a woman haunted by things that forced her to sleep in a stranger's house. She wasn't someone spinning tales about a childhood in 1914. She wasn't a siren who bent his mind with her sweet song. She was just a girl standing under the night sky, wrapped in moonlight and the soft glow of the streetlamps. She held his hand. Her eyes lit up when they met his.

Hunter didn't know what to do with that kind of normal. It felt like a new kind of spell, and he was not prepared for it. If he allowed himself to love something so ordinary, then Sarah might be lost to him completely. His heart might run out of room as he moved through days filled with work and nights spent with friends, while Olivia stayed by his side, always holding on. There would be no more promises to chase her into the forest. There would be no moment of being swallowed by a tree while she clung to him, preserving their pain, their grief, and their love. That world would no longer be possible.

"There he is. Hunter!" a high-pitched voice yelled over the speakers playing orchestrated holiday music.

"Here we go," Hunter muttered to Olivia, who squeezed his hand tighter, the smile on her face growing. There was a pulse of excitement around her, and Hunter found it infectious as his mood lightened, his social anxiety ebbed, and he found comfort and security in the person's hand that he held.

You're mine. I'm yours.

Nina stood in front of the caramel popcorn stand, her arm looped through that of a tall, lanky blond man who waved so energetically it drew a few curious glances from passing fairgoers. The warm scent of butter and sugar drifted around them, mixing with the distant squeal of carnival rides and bursts of laughter.

Hunter spotted them just as Darius strolled up, clapping him lightly on the shoulder.

"Hey, man, have you met Tom?" Darius asked, a grin tugging at his mouth.

Nina shot her husband an exasperated look; his deadpan expression betrayed no hint of a joke.

"He's kidding," she said quickly, giving Tom's arm a playful squeeze.

"Hey, Tom," Hunter said with a polite nod, though he wasn't entirely sure what to make of him yet.

A few feet away, Celia and Elaine leaned against the side of a portable table piled with half-empty paper cups and napkins. They chatted quietly, but their conversation fell away as the group grew, both of them glancing up with expectant smiles.

"This is Olivia," Hunter announced. "Olivia, this is everybody."

"Wow, you really brought her." Sadie appeared out of nowhere, her words muffled from the bite of a Bavarian pretzel with stone ground mustard that she'd just taken.

"I'm Nina. Did you just move here?" Nina unhooked her arm from Tom's and started asking Olivia a million questions. Hunter's nerves kicked back in because Olivia's eyes moved elsewhere instead of answering or even looking at the human being talking directly to her.

A carriage moved past on the sidewalk, and a large dark chestnut horse pulled the vintage vehicle, carrying a family who all looked too bored. Bells attached to the horse's reins jingled with every synchronized step, creating a beat to liven up the classical, orchestral music playing throughout the loudspeakers.

Next, her eyes were drawn to the oversized Christmas tree half a mile down the street, displayed on the steps of the town hall, towering high over them all. Olivia frowned, and Hunter wanted more than anything to know her thoughts, to help fix what she thought was wrong, before she took action into her own hands.

"Let's go over to the carousel," Elaine said, slinking towards Olivia, grabbing her other arm like they were best friends. Celia moved with her, and suddenly the three women began walking away in the opposite direction of the Christmas tree, three heads of hair glistening underneath the hanging twinkle lights.

"So, interesting that you're with Hunter," he heard Elaine say. "You seem a little twisted for him."

"Oh, Hunter is a little twisted." Olivia's voice faded as they walked further away.

"Really? I knew it. Tell us more." Celia's excited shriek barely reached his ears before Sadie stood right before him, offering him some of her pretzel.

"What are we supposed to be doing?" Hunter asked his friend. Sadie's short hair seemed even shorter. "Did you get a haircut?"

"Thank you for noticing! I shaved off the sides," she said, her smile wide.

"I would like to see a beer in each of my hands," Darius said. "This is incredibly not fun at all."

Hunter had to agree, though the swirl of noise and movement made it hard to think. Hundreds of people streamed past them in every direction. Somewhere behind him, a child wailed loudly enough to pierce through the chatter. A couple near the kettle corn stand hissed arguments at each other under their breath, holiday sweaters bright as sin. He forced himself to nod along, but his eyes kept searching the crowd for Olivia. She was somewhere in this mess, too fragile for all this noise. He couldn't shake the thought that she might disappear again, and no one but him would notice.

"We should have worn matching ugly Christmas sweaters," Nina said, her bottom lip pouting out. "This was not planned very well. Next year I'm taking over."

"I don't have an ugly Christmas sweater." Hunter shrugged. "And I probably didn't have enough time to go get one."

"You could have borrowed one of Tom's," Nina said as if it were the most obvious thing in the world.

Tom did not look enthused.

"Let's go get Darius that pilsner," Sadie suggested, pointing toward a vendor with a more substantial booth with wooden walls set up to look like a rustic cabin.

"That line is six miles long." Darius frowned.

"I think that's called Christmas spirit." Hunter laughed.

"All of the forced fun," Sadie teased, not meeting Nina's eyes.

"Come on, Tom," Darius said, making Nina's eyes lighten a bit.

As their group trudged through the line, the holiday music on the speakers died down, and a band was setting up in front of the Christmas tree. Hunter saw a trombone, an electric guitar, a set of drums, and a saxophone gleaming from the decorations on the tree.

"At least the music is going to get more lively." Hunter motioned toward the musicians.

"Forty bucks for three beers? I'm a teacher, man." Darius complained to the poor girl working in the window. "Sorry, guys, we are going Dutch."

Darius paid, collected a single twenty-ounce plastic cup filled with a foamy yellow liquid, and let the others move through the window. Hunter went next, collected his alcohol, being the last of their smaller, divided group to not order the hot mug of spiced mule. The cold condensation on his hands after some of his drink bounced over the rim made him regret not ordering something hot, so he began to chug.

"Whoa, there's a lumberjack," Darius laughed. "I know I joked about double fisting, but you're really going for it."

"I just want it out of my hands," Hunter said, gasping for air with only a fifth of the beer left as the others gathered around him. His head immediately got lighter, his shoulders relaxed, and his blood warmed.

"Are they still in line for the carousel?" Sadie asked. "I wanted to get to know this new girl better."

"I'm not happy that she was pulled away from me," Hunter said, eyeing the carousel in the distance, unable to make out any individual people.

"A little possessive, are we, then? Hunter, that's certainly a new side of you I've never seen," Sadie said, sipping her spiced steaming mug and then frowning. "Ooh, that's not good."

Sadie wasn't wrong. Hunter's anxiety had been growing, his fingers throbbing since Olivia's hand was not laced within his.

"The drink helps, but yeah, it's a new relationship, and she's new to the area. I'm a little protective."

"I like tipsy Hunter," Darius said. "He's an entirely more dominant type of man."

"I went to his house yesterday, and I thought she was going to jump on me, attack me; so you know, it could be some of her hostile influence." Sadie snorted.

"I didn't get hostile from her," Nina said, "more whimsical, a woodland fairy."

"With claws," Sadie muttered.

"Let's talk about how jealous you sound." Darius laughed at Sadie.

"I'm not going anywhere, Sadie." Hunter sighed, gulping down the last of his beer. "Let's go explore so I can go home."

"That's the spirit," Darius said, cheering his beer in the air.

"We can head over in that general direction so they can catch up."

The five began walking down the row toward the carousel, vendors smiling and trying to attract customers to their hand-made trinkets. Their pace was slow as they perused hand-knitted scarves, caramel popcorn in ribbon-wrapped jars, and jewelry.

Hunter stopped at one of the tables, picking up a necklace with a moon pendant hanging from a silver chain. It glistened as if it were made of the very snow that threatened to start falling from the sky at any moment, a sheen over the pendant that caught and held onto any light it could pull.

"Spooky necklace," Darius said. "She's into that stuff, then, your new girl? The dark and the ominous?"

"It's just a moon, Darius," Hunter said, but he wasn't wrong; it did remind him of Olivia.

"I'll take this," he said, holding it up to the vendor. He then handed over some cash before moving on.

"Oh my gosh," Nina squealed. "Look at those ornaments. Tiny reindeer made out of walnuts. I wonder if I can make this an art project for the kindergartners next year."

"I think suggesting that five-year-olds can make what someone is trying to sell can be defeating," Hunter heard Tom say.

"Tom's kind of a dick, no?" Darius lowered his voice.

Hunter nodded.

"We don't need any more ornaments, Nina. The tree already looks like it has exploded," Tom said as Nina moved onto another vendor table, lifting a glittery snowflake.

"But these are so festive." Her smile didn't suggest that she realized that Tom was a dick.

"So was the glitter avalanche last year. I was still finding sparkles in my socks in late March." Tom moved over to Hunter and Darius, his eyebrows raised as if he were joking with a group of his friends.

"I'm sorry, are you talking to us?" Darius just went for it, Tom's head drooping as he moved back to stand by Nina.

"Glitter never leaves. It haunts you forever, like taxes or ghosts," Sadie said, grimacing while forcing down another drink.

"You don't have to finish that," Hunter said.

"This? Oh no, this was twenty dollars. You are very mistaken. I absolutely do have to finish it."

Darius moved up to the next vendor, huffing and puffing.

"Here we go," Sadie muttered.

"Ethically sourced alpaca wool? What does that mean exactly?" Darius wasn't yelling at the vendor, but his voice was raised enough for Hunter to hear everything he was saying clearly. "Did the alpaca get a say?"

Sadie ran up and pushed him back, his hands dropping the smock he held up. "Darius, we talked about this. No activism at the holiday market."

Sadie, always caring too much.

"I'm just saying." Darius turned toward her. "Last year's protest got us a lot of attention."

Hunter chuckled at the memory. "You mean when you chained yourself to the Christmas tree displayed at the town square? That tree had already been cut, Darius."

"It's about the message. That tree was not sustainably harvested," Darius said, bending the now empty plastic cup in his hand. They were all getting a little flustered by the alcohol in their blood.

Hunter just needed to keep moving forward, towards where he knew Olivia to be last. They had been apart for too long.

"You know, Darius, you and Olivia might actually get along," Hunter said, gently pushing Darius along.

"Oh really? She's into activism, too?"

"Not exactly, but she's really into trees."

"Guys! Guys! Gingerbread house contest, right now!" Nina yelled, grabbing Tom by the hand and running through a group of teenagers who were very much judging her enthusiasm.

Hunter tried to look over the cluster of heads and bouncing Santa hats, searching for a glimpse of shiny black hair that might catch the moonlight—or, under this tent, the harsh glow of Christmas lights strung too bright and too low. Sadie nudged him firmly, steering him toward the larger open tent to his left. Inside, rows of tables were covered with candy bowls and cookie pieces, and volunteers in bright red Santa hats offered forced, tired smiles to the crowd.

"Nina, the last time you turned this into a contest, you nearly filed for divorce over a sandcastle," Tom said. He ducked slightly under a sagging string of plastic mistletoe that brushed his hair.

"For someone so sweet and small, she is oddly competitive," Darius added. He stood just behind Tom, arms crossed, his winter coat streaked with powdered sugar from who knew what.

Nina ignored them both and dropped into the nearest seat. She grabbed a stack of hard gingerbread panels as if she planned to build a real house, not a candy version destined to collapse. "You refused to commit to the turret, Tom. Do not rewrite history."

Sadie laughed and rested her elbow on Hunter's shoulder. "Should we be worried? Is your marriage at the mercy of gingerbread and icing this year?"

Tom shot her a flat look, then turned to Hunter. "If you could just make something truly terrible, I would owe you. It might save me from a long car ride full of gloating."

Hunter forced a grin, though his mind drifted to the tent entrance. He could not help searching for Olivia. Somewhere out there, Celia and Elaine were probably trying to keep her calm or distracted. He should have been beside her, not stuck pretending he could joke about Christmas like everyone else.

"Don't drag me into your domestic warfare," Hunter said, hoping his voice did not sound as strained as he felt.

Sadie pushed away from him and pointed a finger at Nina. "I am going to build a gingerbread mansion. It will be art. It will be iconic."

Nina did not even look up. Her hands moved so fast that gumdrops and peppermint bark scattered onto the table. She pressed icing along every seam with the precision of a surgeon.

"She's just as scary as your haunted forest, Hunter," Sadie said, wagging her eyebrows.

Hunter managed a laugh. He could still feel the tight knot in his chest where Christmas used to sit warm and easy. Sarah had made this season feel like peace. Now it was noise, obligation, and small talk that did not fill the space she'd left behind.

"My gingerbread house will be eco-friendly," Darius declared. He claimed the spot across from Nina and began stacking pieces without any clear plan. "It will reflect the harsh reality of deforestation."

Hunter shook his head. "So, just a sad pile of crumbs, then?"

Darius pointed at him with a piece of peppermint stick. "It is called minimalism. Also, it is called helping my best friend escape this nonsense as quickly as possible."

Hunter appreciated him for that. Darius always had a quiet way of protecting everyone without smothering them.

He sank into a slate-gray folding chair and made sure he could see the tent entrance clearly. He tried to tune out Nina barking orders at Tom, who looked like he regretted every life choice that had brought him to this table. Sadie hummed while smearing frosting across a roof that sagged dangerously. Darius poked at his crumbling pile as if it might fix itself if he stared hard enough.

He should have been doing this with Sarah. They would have laughed at their crooked walls and eaten half the candy before finishing the roof. He wondered if she would hate how he clung to this ghost version of her every Christmas.

"Use more icing, Darius. More is better," Nina shouted, sounding like a drill sergeant covered in sugar.

"My roof is sliding off," Sadie said. She pressed her lips together and looked at her disaster.

Nina slapped her hands on the table. "You did not brace the walls properly. That is basic gingerbread physics."

Hunter raised an eyebrow at her. "Why do you look personally insulted by poor construction?"

Darius sighed. "This is why the world needs sustainable architecture. Less heartbreak, fewer broken roofs."

Sadie threw up her hands. "Can I just drown my walls in frosting without getting a lecture from the holiday tyrant?"

Nina ignored her. Minutes later, her own gingerbread masterpiece buckled and collapsed in a sticky heap. Her cheeks flushed as red as her Santa hat. Hunter half-expected her to flip the entire table, and part of him wished she would.

"Someone get that angry little elf a drink," Sadie muttered. She ducked when Nina swatted at her arm. "It is not that serious, I promise."

Hunter stood as the group filed out of the tent, the cold air biting at the heat building under his collar. Snow drifted down, settling in his hair and lashes until he blinked it away. This time of year used to feel like hope. Now, it just reminded him how much he had lost.

"Time for another beer," Darius said, leading the charge back into the fairgrounds. Sadie muttered something about donuts and hurried after him.

Hunter stopped short when he saw Olivia. She walked

toward him with Celia and Elaine on either side, all three of them dark silhouettes against the glitter of lights and fresh snow. Elaine hooked her arm through Olivia's and called out over the chatter.

"Your girlfriend is a prize, Hunter. Honestly, she could do so much better, so worship the ground she walks on."

Relief cracked through his chest like a breath of warm air. He looked into Olivia's dark eyes, the only thing that made him feel steady in all this chaos.

"Do not worry," Hunter said. He stepped forward and let Olivia catch his hand. "I already do."

18

CHAPTER EIGHTEEN.

"We stood behind a group of people for a long time. Most of them were very young, crying because there was no whipped cream on the hot chocolate," Olivia told Hunter with her hand back in his. As Nina and Tom bickered about the gingerbread house debacle, their group marched through the holiday market.

Where was the trick, the hidden agenda? There was too much potential for Hunter to feel happy, or dare he say even normal. Here he was, with his coworkers, some he even considered friends, and a girlfriend, dare he say, that he was holding onto tightly.

"There was a sickeningly happy song playing repeatedly while a giant machine adorned with horrifying statues of animals spun in a circle. When we got to the front of the line, we sat on those animal statues. Mine was a whimsical sheep that was absolutely deranged, its eyes dead and its smile too large."

"I told you she was awesome," Celia said, her black skirt swishing as she and Elaine skipped up ahead.

This is going well. You can relax.

The town square was at the end of the street, and they were headed right toward it, passing new vendors. Darius stopped to get another beer. Hunter offered Olivia one, which she immediately crinkled her nose at, but seemed entirely more interested in the hot roasted cashews that Sadie forced them to pull over for.

The band near the Christmas tree was taking down their setup as a women's choir wearing all black, bundled up in puffy jackets, took over the area. They arranged themselves in rows as people below the steps huddled together to watch.

"I've probably got another half an hour in me, then I'm going to head out," Darius announced, his steps getting a little wobbly.

"How about you let me get you a driver to take you home, my man," Hunter said. "We can all band together and make sure everyone gets their cars in the morning if they need to leave them here."

"We don't drink and are happy to help carpool," Nina chipped in.

"Does she expect an award?" Sadie muttered, mouth clenched, on Hunter's free side.

"Play nice, Sadie." Hunter nudged her, pulling Olivia into him as his weight shifted.

"So, Olivia, what do you do?" Darius asked, nodding toward Hunter.

He appreciated the subject change. There was an odd hostility lingering in the air, and, funnily enough, it didn't have anything to do with the woman he thought he had dug a grave for earlier in the day.

He could feel it pressing at the edges of his patience, but when he looked at her, he realized it wasn't her fault. Any frustration he had existed only in the questions he didn't have answers for. It surprised him, this lack of blame. He wasn't sure if it made him a fool or something worse. Either way, changing the subject felt easier than explaining any of it out loud.

"She just moved here, Darius; give a girl some room to breathe," Elaine said, her voice airy, cool, and unbothered as she looked up at the sky.

"I take care of trees." Olivia surprised Hunter by engaging. He hadn't heard her say much to anyone else that wasn't him. Elaine and Celia seemed to make her comfortable, then.

"You're an arborist? That is honestly the most amazing thing I think I've ever heard." Darius's face broke out in pure amazement, a child filled with hopes and dreams on Christmas morning. "Are you looking for work? Who hires arborists? Is it the city?"

Olivia blinked at him in the way she did while their group continued to walk past more stands, more tables filled with the late-night crowd who appeared with too many mules already in their bellies.

"Olivia is more of a soloist, aren't you?" Hunter smiled.

She nodded.

"Ah, an entrepreneur. How fetching. You're making me jealous, Olivia. I need to dream bigger."

Darius sighed.

"Don't sell yourself short," Celia said, walking a few steps in front of them. "You're young, you're attractive, you're obnoxiously passionate. Just be careful not to wallow; you attract the same energy you put into the world. Oops, sorry, Hunter."

"Sorry for what?" Hunter's attention was elsewhere, staring down at Olivia's hand in his, at the way her finger rubbed little circles around the outside of his thumb.

"I think Hunter is attracting the exact attention that he needs." Olivia's sweet voice coated his ears.

I certainly am.

"Ooooh, Hunter and Olivia kissing in a tree," Sadie started dancing.

"K-I-S-S-I-N-G," Nina joined in, her head bobbing like a maniac.

Hunter and Olivia smiled at each other. He laughed as she looked down awkwardly, not knowing how to handle the attention and energy, despite how playful it was. They were awfully loud.

"It's easy to tell you all work with children." Elaine rolls her eyes.

At least they're not making fun of me about pickles today.

"Watch out for his pickle, Olivia!" Sadie spat her laughter out.

I stand corrected.

"These are friends?" Olivia looked at him, genuinely asking.

"Unfortunately, I would argue that I have better friends than most."

New light patterns hit the pavement under their feet as they approached the towering Christmas tree in the town square. Their pace slowed even further as a crowd gathered to listen to the choir, and judging by the conductor raising her hands and framing an overextended jaw, pointing to the roof of her mouth, they were about to start.

"Sarah would have loved that tree," Sadie said out of nowhere.

"Why would you say that?" Hunter didn't get an answer as an eruption of music weaved all around them, the staccato notes harmonizing with a sole male tenor who walked up to stand by the female conductor. Her hands waved so dramatically that it seemed like a joke.

"Ding, dong, ding, dong."

"Oh," Olivia gasped. "This song."

"Are you okay?" Hunter asked, feeling her arm tighten against him. He looked over at her, her face matching someone's who could fall apart at any moment.

"This is my song. Our song," Olivia muttered.

The choir's onomatopoeias turned into lyrics.

"Hark, how the bells
Sweet silver bells"

"Our song?" Hunter tried to keep her talking, keep her breathing. The tenseness that was in her body a moment ago suddenly fled as she fell limp against him.

"My dad. It's why he's dead. This song."

"Aw, your dad died? I'm so sorry, honey," Nina interjected as Olivia started to shake.

Hunter had heard her sing it before, more than once, but he'd never considered it meant anything specific to her, other than being a Christmas song from long ago. Most of the ones he knew were a bit more modern.

"Olivia, you don't have to fall apart. I'm here, I've got you," he whispered in her ear. Unfortunately, that did not help, as a flood of tears soaked her cheeks, the salty water reflecting greens, whites, and golds from the lights on the tree, the garlands, and the street lamps.

She was a painted doll, filled with sadness, a moon who was grieving.

A moon.

Hunter remembered his gift and pulled the necklace from his jacket pocket, wrapped in blue tissue paper.

"This reminded me of you. I wanted you to have it," he said, holding it out to her. She didn't look at it; her eyes focused on the choir and the song that continued. Hunter could see a memory playing out on her face, something horrific, the day her world fell apart.

Olivia reached out and placed her hand on top of Hunter's in order to grab the necklace. She gripped it hard, her fist so tight.

"All seem to say
Throw cares away

Ding, dong, ding, dong
That is the song."

He had no notice, no training, no idea how to respond as it unfolded. Olivia's lips twitched and tears streamed steadily down her face. Hunter's coworkers looked at her, some concerned, some stepping awkwardly back, bumping into random bystanders who had closed in behind their small group.

She sang. She sang with them.

"Hawk, how the bells
Sweet Silver Bells."

Olivia's song looped in harmony with theirs. Her voice was soft at first, but as she continued, it grew louder. Nervous faces turned to look at her.

No, not nervous, scared, compliant.

The familiar haze that coaxed Hunter into a state of happy, blind obedience, that convinced him that what he wanted to do more than anything else was what Olivia commanded, snuck its way back into his mind.

The spell of the song, the magic in her voice, dropped any personality from the crowd's gazes, expressions now empty and vacant. Hunter's mind continued to fight and recognized that intrusive magic was invading, an unwelcome guest.

This wasn't intentional. Hunter sensed that instantly. Unlike her song in his home when he had buried the TV, Hunter could hold on to consciousness, though he felt it slipping a little more with every breath, a rope he desperately hung onto as he climbed up a cliff engulfed in thick, eerie fog.

He took in his group of friends. Darius had straightened up like a soldier waiting for orders. Nina and Tom had their heads tilted like living dolls in a horror movie, nothing behind their stares. Elaine and Celia looked nearly the same, though there was something different about their lips—less defiance, less of a grimace at the corners of their mouths.

He wondered if he looked like any of them, or if he had more awareness. No one was looking at him, no one noticed that he was glancing around, but the entire crowd had now turned away from the choir, their attention on her, on Olivia with the moon and stars in her hair, with the necklace Hunter had given her still squeezed in her hand.

Olivia choked between sobs, but continued to sing. However, one by one, the choir fell under her spell. Hunter could focus on her voice, the overpowering vibrato coming from the group fading more and more until they were merely background singers.

This was Olivia's show now.

"I'm still here," Hunter said, and the words took substantial effort. Pushing past that haze that wanted him blank, in a state of walking sleep, felt like a superpower, something unnatural that he shouldn't be able to do.

But he was there.

Here I am.

"You're mine," he stammered.

Olivia didn't hear, or at least she didn't react. Her song continued on a loop as she started singing it again from the top.

"All seem to say,

Throw cares away,

Christmas is here,

Bringing good cheer."

There was a gasp of air as she threw her head back toward the sky. Her hair took the shape of a crescent moon while she threw her hands behind her and screamed at the darkness overhead. Hunter watched it all in slow motion.

Snow landed on her cheeks. Frost clung to her devastatingly beautiful eyelashes. Her mouth was open as she howled. Olivia's pain wrecked its way through everyone's ears in a supernaturally loud yet pulchritudinous caterwaul.

My tree siren.

Tree siren she was, as anything green or rooted reacted to her noise, to her grief, breaking open the gates of hell on the surface of the Earth.

Hunter couldn't respond; that haze still had such a hold of him.

What he wanted to do was grab Olivia and shield her, so that he could take the brunt of what was coming. Instead, he stood there, his body dazed, nearly paralyzed, rooted down as if the earth had decayed the pavement and wrapped itself around his feet.

It might as well have done that, the terror already clawed through him, as Olivia's cry threatened to cover downtown Stockbridge so that it may never see the sun again.

At least, that was Hunter's initial reaction when the Christmas tree behind the carolers lashed out each branch, growing hundreds of feet and crashing down onto the large group of immobile spectators wearing their holiday best, stuck under Olivia's spell.

There were no screams. The group nearly welcomed it.

It was grief made manifest. A heartbroken woman unleashed the storm she could no longer hold inside.

She couldn't help it. It was who she was.

Hunter knew it was his choice, but it was certainly a choice to stay in her heart as violence broke out in the calmest manner, a true, cheerful holiday horror.

Thwap. Thwap.

The tree branches whipped at the crowd, catching their victims and wrapping them from head to toe in silken webs spun of pine and pressure. He could see red pooling, blood a dark crimson mixed with the green.

He could not tell if the pine was driving into his skin or if the branches were simply wrapped too tightly around him. The haze pressed harder against his throat and swelled inside him like something alive and angry. It wanted to choke out any words he might have left. It felt like a punishment for daring to speak at all.

He thought her name as if she could hear it.

Olivia. Help. Please.

She was still crying. Her body shook so violently that her knees hit the ground. Something inside her had broken open. She was not ready for this. She was not ready for any of it. And now, the world cracked beneath the weight of her unraveling. He would carry it if he had to.

Is this how it all ends, Sarah?

He knew he had moved on too fast. He could see it now with painful clarity. The blame belonged to him and him alone. He had dragged Olivia out of the forest when he should have left her to its shadows and silence. There had been a terrible comfort in the darkness back then, a quiet promise that wherever his wife had gone, he could follow and disappear alongside her.

But he had refused that surrender. He had insisted on pretending to be a hero because he needed to matter to someone living. He'd needed someone to save so he would not drown in the memory of saving no one at all.

Now, Sarah was not the only one whose soul had tangled with his. He had allowed it to happen again, and he could not decide which shamed him more—wanting it or lying to himself that he did not.

He would fight for his life now because of Olivia. She needed him in ways he did not fully understand. She was a monster, something wild and untamed, maybe even dangerous enough to kill him without meaning to. Yet she was real. She made him real, too.

The thought cut through him, sharp and cold, but it did not leave. He was tired of being the broken man that people pitied and spoke around. He wanted to be something steadier, something good, the way his father had always been for his mom. But Olivia was not his mom. She was not soft laughter in a safe kitchen or quiet weekends spent folding laundry. Olivia was a storm. She was a beast that no one could hold down.

The haze began to lift from his chest. Air filled his lungs again, rough and cold but precious. Around him, the low hum of panic rose into clearer voices. The crowd was waking up. He was still here to hear it.

Was she stopping? Was she pulling back?

"Olivia," Hunter growled out, but he still couldn't reach out his hand, the haze still gripping his body despite feeling like each stitch of an invisible binding fabric was individually breaking open, one at a time.

The garland that hung between the streetlamps slithered down to the pavement, taking over the ground and tugging on ankles so that people fell face-first into asphalt, wrapping them in vines like children's paper chains, tightening but not yet tearing.

"You have to stop. Olivia, you're killing them all."

Her face was buried in her hands. Hunter wasn't sure if she even knew what was happening.

A branch from the Christmas tree thwacked past him, and his stomach leapt.

Fear.

That was good; he could feel fear. His body had the instinct to survive through the haze.

Fog poured into the square without warning, as if someone had dumped dry ice into every storm drain at once. It carried a strange, unnatural weight that pressed against Hunter's chest and rooted him in place. Whatever force crackled in the air around him made it impossible to feel the fog on his bare skin. It moved in slow, greedy waves from every corner of the square, thick and wet, clinging to clothes and creeping into hair like the smell of rot.

Within the dense mist, the town's lights burned with a sickly yellow-green glow, their shapes distorted by something that did not want to be seen. Every strand of Christmas bulbs along the storefronts flickered in fits and starts, struggling to stay alive. Their colors had turned dark and swollen, bruised like dead flesh left too long in the cold.

The garlands coiled tighter around a man's legs as he screamed for help. They dragged him across the street, his body scraping over the rough pavement. His fingernails caught on the asphalt, tearing away and leaving jagged red smears behind him.

A few people lunged forward to help, but no one reached him in time.

But the vines paused, shivering in place as if confused. The garlands trembled with Olivia's wavering will, squeezing, but not shredding. His screams turned to sobs. He was still breathing. The spell was shifting.

Hunter stumbled back and nearly fell as his boot caught on a rogue vine that had broken through a storm drain. The air buzzed around him, not with insects but with a kind of electricity, a hum that resonated in his bones and teeth. It felt static, like the anger and wrath his TV would express after its unfortunate burial.

Olivia knelt in the middle of the street, her shoulders trembling. Around her, the asphalt cracked and heaved. From those ruptures, green things were blooming. Not the soft green of spring, but a sickly, hungry color—glossy leaves slick with sap that dripped like saliva.

"Olivia," Hunter said again, quieter this time, as if volume might shatter her more. "Look at me. Please."

She didn't, but her sobs were calming down, her shuddering less violent.

To his left, the Christmas tree at the center of the square stood tall and glittering, a beautiful icon wrapped in delicate silver tinsel. It let out a deep, creaking groan that cut through the quiet night. A second groan followed, louder and more strained. The trunk began to bulge in uneven swells, as if something hidden inside was struggling to push its way out. Without warning, the bark split open—not in a clean line down the center, but in a jagged, pulsing wound that seemed to breathe in the cold air.

From that wound, thick red vines spilled out. They were wet, veiny tendrils tipped with spines and dripping with a crimson secretion that steamed as it touched the ground.

Hunter gagged.

The vines lashed out, striking faster than he could track. One pierced the undercarriage of a car, lifting it off its wheels and flinging it like a toy. Another impaled a man in a Santa suit, pinning him to a light post where his body twitched and bled into the snow-dusted ground.

People scattered in every direction. Some ran screaming down narrow alleyways, their footsteps lost beneath the rising roar of the shifting trees. Others stood rooted to the spot, eyes wide, trapped in a terror they couldn't look away from.

A woman grabbed her toddler's arm and pulled, but the vines had already begun to creep up the child's boots. They coiled, but hesitated, then slowly unwrapped and recoiled into the earth. The child sobbed but was thankfully unharmed.

The entire town square was transforming. The quaint buildings lining the streets, brick cafés and boutiques with wreaths in the windows, were being overtaken. Ivy broke through walls. Thorned vines crawled through shattered glass and pulled mannequins from displays like corpses from coffins. One of them dangled, spinning slowly, a red scarf now coiled like a noose.

The law enforcement vehicle crash seemed so innocent, a dream, compared to this. How the town would ever recover, he didn't know.

Hunter crouched low and ducked behind a ruined bench, heart pounding. Something brushed his neck. He swatted it away and saw a sprig of holly on his shoulder, its leaves gleaming like metal. Blood oozed from three fresh puncture wounds in his skin.

He bit back a scream and pressed forward. He had to get to Olivia.

She stood now, with her arms resting loosely at her sides and her head tilted back toward the dark sky. Each breath escaped her mouth in soft clouds of steam. There was something different about her expression, something calmer yet distant. Her lips moved in a steady rhythm, forming words meant for something or someone no one else could see. The lights that surrounded her no longer flickered unpredictably. Instead, they pulsed in and out, steady as a heartbeat, perfectly in time with her own.

The garlands and vines moved around her like dancers. Or worshippers.

"Olivia!" he yelled again.

Her head turned slowly, and some recognition finally appeared in those dark eyes. Hunter felt like he was looking into a black hole that he had fallen into and would never be able to come back out of, even if he wanted to.

"I didn't mean for this to happen," she said, voice dreamy, distant.

"These are people, Olivia. They're dying!"

"No killing during Christmas," she whispered and nodded, like a child who remembered something that had been forgotten.

A new sound slithered through the cold air, a low and steady creaking that rose and fell like the grinding of ancient wooden gears. Behind Olivia, the Christmas tree shuddered once, then began to move again. This time it did not crawl. It rose. The roots at its base tore free from the frozen soil, unfurling like dozens of crooked legs searching for balance. The trunk swelled and twisted, growing thicker with each groan of wood and snapping branch. One by one, the delicate ornaments burst apart, falling away to reveal what they had hidden: pale bones tangled in dried flowers, shards of brittle hair, and rows of human teeth embedded deep within the bark.

It had a face.

Not a real face, but something that mimicked one—branches bent into eye sockets, strands of tinsel clumped together into a grinning, jagged maw. And it was watching.

Hunter took a step back. "What the hell is that?"

Olivia didn't answer.

The tree screamed.

It was not a sound meant for ears. It was deep and shrill at once, like every dying animal on Earth screaming from one throat.

Windows exploded.

Light bulbs burst in their sockets.

People clutched their heads, blood running from their noses and ears.

Hunter dropped to the ground. The air was too loud to breathe.

Shhhhhhhh.

There was a hush.

He opened his eyes, and the square, once a cheerful holiday celebration, was now a garden of blood. The fog cleared, and Olivia smiled, radiant, a goddess.

"No killing during Christmas," she repeated. "If I'd had that rule before, maybe things could have been different."

19

CHAPTER NINETEEN.

"We need to go."

Hunter couldn't process the words at first, until Darius repeated himself, pushing Hunter and reaching for Elaine.

Where did he come from?

Olivia stared at him, eyes bright, hopeful, even. What she was hoping for, what she expected from him right then and there, he didn't know. He didn't even think he could guess.

Screams. Hunter heard screams.

"Roger, wake up, help!" a woman cried.

"Has anyone seen Tom? Tom, where are you?"

Nina.

That was Nina stumbling around, checking the unmoving bodies on the ground. There must have been dozens. Hunter couldn't look at them. He had to disassociate, choosing instead to focus on the woman with the moon necklace in her hand.

"We need to go," Darius said again. This time, Hunter took a few steps forward from the pressure pushing against him, instinctively reaching out and grabbing Olivia's hand. She wouldn't be left behind. Not by him.

"What happened?" Elaine cried out, her cool-girl demeanor crumpling as her face twisted from holding back tears. "I don't ... I don't understand."

Hunter heard sirens in the distance growing louder as the seconds passed.

"Are you okay?" Celia stumbled towards Olivia, pushing Hunter back. "Elaine, Elaine, are you okay?"

"I can't find Tom." Nina was hunched over bodies, lifting their heads, blood on her hands that wasn't hers. "Tom! You need to finish the turret, come back."

No one knows.

"I think we are past worrying about drunk driving, but does anyone want a ride home?" Sadie made her way back to their group in the middle of the town square.

Hunter spun slowly in place. His ears rang. The world felt tilted, unreconciled with what had just happened. A minute ago, they were in a massacre. Now the Christmas tree sparkled innocently, the garlands were perfectly strung, the lights a bright, gleaming red. The vines were gone. The crowd was murmuring, confused but mobile. Some people dusted snow off their coats as if they'd just woken from a nap.

But the bodies were still there. He wasn't crazy. He wasn't making it up.

AND YET—EVERYTHING looked normal again. Why?

Olivia looked too calm. As if this was just a detour, an accidental mess at a holiday event.

SHE SHOOK her head while Hunter's coworkers and friends asked her if she had been hurt.

Of course, she wasn't hurt. She was the weapon there. And all she did was cry.

"If I'd had that rule before, maybe things could have been different."

That's what she had said to him. She had been grieving her father, her childhood, her life. The song had triggered her. Hunter had heard her sing that song before, a song that existed in both of their timelines.

Of course, this would trigger her.

And maybe ... maybe she had been hurt long before she ever hurt anyone.

He remembered what life had been like just a few days ago —drifting, numb, invisible even to the people who claimed to know him best.

HE COULDN'T GO BACK.

But this? He could do this.

Can I really?

No one had protected her.

OLIVIA WASN'T A MONSTER. She was someone whose life had been cruel enough to teach her to cry alone.

If Hunter was going to live in a world where he accepted that the supernatural was real then he could live in a world where he could protect her from herself. An accidental outburst, ending innocent lives, would be a part of his own now.

Ding.

Ping.

Zaaap.

Bop.

The sound of phones lighting up with activity filled the air.

"Shit," said Darius. "We're taking too long."

Hunter pulled out his phone from his pocket, wiping off

smeared blood from the camera lens. Suddenly, his phone started to vibrate in his hand, and the sounds of text messages turned into a nightmare as a piercing alarm echoed through the entire block. He went to silence it, the alert only dying down when he read what was on the screen.

Emergency Alert

Main Street Stockbridge

Contamination units are on their way.

"Holy shit," Sadie looked like she was about to throw up.

"This is what I've been trying to say. There are a slew of dead bodies on the ground. Everyone will be kept here for questioning, and who knows what else."

Darius was right. They had to run.

The sirens were so loud that they sounded only a block away, and Hunter could hear the slamming of the van doors and the sound of dress shoes and heels clicking away from the news reporters, who had somehow arrived there quicker than anyone who could actually help.

"Let's go." Hunter grabbed Olivia by the wrist and tugged, running out of the square, knowing his friends were behind him.

He saw a police car rushing down the block.

"Shit," he yelled, "Duck down!"

They moved behind some trash cans, not the best hiding spot, but in the commotion, it did the trick, as no one noticed them or stopped them.

"Nina isn't here," Celia said as they stood up to keep going. "We have to make sure she's safe."

"There's no time," Darius said. "She's looking for Tom. They got separated. She wouldn't come with us."

"We can't just leave her behind," Celia yelled.

Olivia looked over at Celia, her face a portrait of calm, her eyes sparkling. "Yes, we can."

Celia's face dropped, mesmerized momentarily before she matched Olivia's slight smile and nodded. Olivia's calm was infectious. Their group was on its way down the block again.

A helicopter flew overhead, a spotlight shining down in the dark that moved over them. Hunter might have had a heart attack then, but he kept going. A few people fleeing a dangerous scene were hopefully all they looked like.

That is all we are, Hunter reminded himself, his thumb massaging Olivia's hand as he tugged a little more gently this time. She had no problem keeping up. Adrenaline pumped through them as they played duck and hide behind this building, or "Quick, in this alleyway," every time they saw a flash of red or blue.

We will be okay. You can protect her.

Hunter was growing more and more confident in this, knowing that he could, knowing that if she was a murderer then he was one as well, and they would go down in history together. Stories would be written about them, the lore of the estate might change, and the tour guides would have something new and modern to tell.

He smiled, knowing his adult life was tied to that manor in more than one significant way.

Once they were a few more blocks away, they saw an occasional person out on the street, someone driving their vehicle without panicking. There were no more emergency rescue vehicles, so they slowed down and stopped. All of them were panting, and Sadie was wheezing. She was older than them, too old for this, really.

"Did anyone see what happened?" Hunter asked, Olivia's eyes widened in surprise at first, but she did a good job at masking that quickly.

"That's the weird thing," Elaine jumped in quickly, cocking

her head. "It feels like I was in a dream, and now that I've woken up, I can barely remember it."

"There was singing," Celia said. "I remember singing."

"That was the choir," Sadie said. "Hunter, what do you remember?"

Hunter made a show of smacking his lips and looking down at the ground as if he were trying to grasp onto memories that were fading away. "I remember comforting Olivia, and then I blinked, and people were on the ground. It was … horrible."

"I'm sorry, Hunter, seeing death like that must be extremely hard on you," Darius said softly.

"Why would it be more so for him?" Elaine scoffed, pulling out her phone. "I'm calling a car. I can't be here."

"Because his late wife was found dead on the ground in her lab," Sadie blurted.

Subtle.

"Hearing it so bluntly is not exactly helping." Hunter sighed. Olivia put her arms around his torso and nuzzled her head against his chest. He wrapped his arms around her.

He couldn't think about Sarah right now.

"We can talk about something else," said Sadie, changing the subject.

"What about Nina and Tom?" Darius pointed out.

"I'll text her," Celia said solemnly.

"What's wrong?" Sadie asked.

"I just, I just have a bad feeling about Tom."

Silence followed, and heads nodded. Tom's being missing wasn't a good sign.

"I don't think she found him in those bodies," Hunter said, trying to comfort but failing. He wasn't good at receiving sympathy over grief, and somehow that now made him unable to give it. This was who he had to be moving forward now. Someone strong, someone who could take care of someone like her.

Someone who could accept that people he knew would die and he would brush it off, pretending that he was surprised, shocked, that he had no idea what had happened. The alternative was one that he couldn't accept: Olivia locked up, studied, poked and prodded like the dead frogs that Darius was sent by the school district once a year for dissection.

If the trees rejected something as simple as a television, what would happen to the world if the human they had bonded with vanished altogether?

Hunter's throat felt like it was going to close up, thinking of Olivia in that position. Hurt, scared, confused. It didn't matter if she could take an entire town out with her tears because at the end of the day, her heart, her soul would still be in pain.

I can't have that.

Seeing that grave in his front lawn had done something to him. It was true that there hadn't turned out to be a body in it, but at first, he had expected it, accepted it and was ready to move on knowing that someone's heart and blood would forever decay under the tree that Olivia made him work so hard to please.

A silver Toyota Corolla pulled up as if it had appeared by magic, and Hunter nearly yelled out.

You're too jumpy. You need to be less emotional for her.

"There's our car," Elaine said, pulling Celia towards the vehicle. She nearly ran toward it, missing Elaine's touch altogether. Elaine turned back. "Do you want a ride, Olivia?"

"She's with me," Hunter nearly growled at the offer. He was surprised at how personally he took that. Elaine was a girl's girl; he knew that. He should be thankful that someone else was looking out for Olivia.

"Are you sure?" Elaine ignored Hunter, his blood boiling a little more, but the pent-up anxiety leaving his chest as Olivia nodded.

"I'm sure I'll see you again," Olivia said, urging the two to get in the car and leave.

"My ride is almost here too," Darius said, pulling out his phone to check his app.

"Mind if I join?" Sadie asked. "I live just a few blocks down from you."

More cars pulled up until no one from their small runaway group was left. Hunter and Olivia were back on his front lawn, staring at the grave and the tree.

"You lied." Olivia turned to him. "You lied to protect me. Why?"

"I think it's self-explanatory," Hunter said.

"Tell me anyway."

Hunter let silence fall between them as he took her face, lips, and jawline. She was so beautiful.

And lethal, like holly at Christmastime.

"Because every second since you came into my life has changed me. You've made me want to become someone better —someone who can hold you when you cry, who wipes your tears gently enough that the plants won't feel the need to protect you so fiercely. When you touch them and feel joy, when you smile ... that brings me peace, too.

You've lived so long in the dark—hiding in a forest where even the sky was out of reach. But you don't have to hide anymore. I know what that feels like. I've done more than my share of it.

I've never met anyone I wanted to bring light to, not until you. And if you'd let me, I'd spend every day—every moment— finding new ways to heal your heart. Because you deserve more than darkness, Olivia. You deserve everything."

Olivia's lip quivered before she bit down on it.

"You have to kiss me now," she said.

And Hunter did.

He kissed her so deeply that he might never come back up for air again.

20

CHAPTER TWENTY.

Olivia's back was pushed against the back of the front door as she let out a slight yelp, followed by a giggle. Hunter thought he might lose his mind. He loved those noises that slipped out of her. A glimpse into her mind, her soul, every burst of air that pushed sound out of her beautiful mouth was a declaration to him that she was his as he was hers.

Hunter didn't have the time or will to question what spell was cast over him, why he was irrevocably obsessed with her, why he would change everything about himself to be stronger for her. It had only been a few days, but he even noticed the tone of danger that developed deep in his throat.

It was her kiss. That was the danger. That kiss whispered seductive hymns of conquering immortality, and that he would have to protect her along the way.

I will.

He knew that. Did she know that now, too?

Hunter fumbled around in his pockets. Olivia's hands seemed to be doing the same. Except she wasn't exactly playing with his pockets. He was stiff as her fingers stroked the shape of his tip.

"Fuck," he nearly nipped at her, burying his face into her neck as he pulled out his keys and, by the grace of God, got it into the keyhole for the first time.

Olivia's right hand moved to the door handle, pressing down as both their bodies, tangled around one another, came tumbling down to the floor. Hunter caught himself, his arm holding himself up in a one-handed plank, the other wrapped under Olivia's head.

"I've been waiting for you to be on top of me," she said, a fire beneath her words that drove Hunter into absolute madness.

He had been waiting for it, too.

Hunter pulled her jacket buttons open with his teeth as she laughed again. "I will pull every single piece of clothing off of your body using my mouth and my hands any time you giggle like that, when you're happy."

"Happy?" Olivia asked, her eyes entertained. "You're thinking of making me happy while I'm underneath you? I think there would be more pressing thoughts going through your mind."

"Oh, there are," he said, smiling and leaning in to place his lips back on hers as they danced a perfect tango—heated, in sync, building with every kiss.

"What are these thoughts?" she asked, coming back up for air, her hands moving to his back as she dug her nails in and slid them down the back of his jacket.

Chills ran through him, from the top of his head down to his feet, and it took everything he had not to pick her up and throw her against the wall. He imagined her moaning, her commanding him to put his hand around her throat as she moaned and writhed, her naked body against his.

He was ready now. He wanted this.

Hunter unleashed himself, giving himself permission to love the woman there before him.

You deserve her.

It felt like a lie still, sand sloshing through his brain as he struggled with the thought.

Maybe not yet, but you will.

"These thoughts are somewhere in the realm of healing more trees, emotionally, of course."

He was joking; there was a twinkle in his eye that made it obvious. Still, Olivia turned her head and swooned, fluttering her eyelashes, a blush creeping up on her cheeks, her chest flushing, and panted breaths getting quicker as if he were truly courting a damsel from the Gilded Age.

She wants you to have her.

Something hit his back, and Hunter nearly jumped out of his skin, but instead, he held himself strong in his plank, protective of Olivia, who had just stared up with a mischievous grin before sticking out her tongue and licking him from his Adam's apple to the underside of his chin, a playful puppy challenging him and distracting him.

"What was that?" he asked, praying that she saw, hoping that Olivia didn't smell the fear that slowly eked out from him. It was funny how closely related grief and fear seemed to him at that moment because Hunter had settled into a life of solicitude other than the awe he had lived in around his tree siren.

Olivia only giggled as that something brushed against him again, this time falling over his right shoulder. It was the mistletoe that they had hung around the ceiling. It seemed to have grown again, needing to touch him, needing to touch her as it fell around her arm and tucked around her cheek.

"It likes you," Olvia said. "It likes that you're an advocate."

I'm an advocate for her. Hunter wanted to correct that statement, to clear up the tender moment so that he could refocus on the two of them, so he could peel the boots and pants off of her. Instead, the mistletoe grew longer and caressed his back again, pulling him down towards her as if they were being tied together with a string.

Before it got too tight, Olivia pushed Hunter up, her hands pressed firmly on his chest with surprising force, as if the mistletoe were holding her up. Hunter looked at the sharp leaves threatening any exposed skin but was flipped over until Olivia was on top, green and red decorating her hair like a crown as it cascaded over her back.

"You are perfect," he felt the words slip his lips. "I can't believe you are real. I can't believe that you're here with me."

"I didn't choose you, Hunter," Olivia said, her legs straddling over his, her ass rubbing against him. "You chose me, with your song. I told you that before. I would follow you if you asked, if you needed, because you are a part of me as I am now a part of you."

Hunter raised his eyes immediately to the wall behind him, trying to blink away tears from the pure acceptance.

It was true, though. He had accepted her fully, and she, in turn, had done the same.

You get a second chance, Hunter. You cannot fuck this up.

Olivia pushed the mistletoe off the top of her head, and it fell willingly. There was no tightness; instead, it slackened. She put her hand on his cheek.

"Oh, Hunter," she said.

He closed his eyes, feeling Olivia's gentle touch. Her pinky finger pulled enough to open his lips, finding its way inside his mouth as Hunter sucked gently, looking at the woman he knew he would forever worship.

Olivia's hands moved off of his face, grabbing his wrists and placing his hands underneath her jacket on her breasts before moving her hips again and biting her lip. She put her cheek to her shoulder as if she were about to let her head fall back, as if she were seconds away from howling at the moon from the window.

He was about to burst. The strength and beauty of the creature—the goddess—on top of him, was more erotic than any movie he could watch, memory he could replay, or book he could read. It was a fantasy, and yet it was real. It was very, very real.

Control yourself, Hunter.

He'd better not blow it before he even got his pants off. Even if she could forgive him, he never would forgive himself. She didn't make it easy, though, as her hips moved to music that he couldn't hear, as her head rolled and her chest swayed in ceremony, in devotion, like a prayer to a divine being that couldn't be touched, seen, or explained by ordinary people like him.

It was entrancing. This time though, there was no haze. She allowed him to be fully present, fully himself.

He looked down, the pressure almost unbearable—his body straining against the confines of his winter pants, every inch of him aching. Need surged through him, raw and insistent, begging for release—for her. To find a home in her heat, where he could stay, moving and pulsing with every breath, every heartbeat, for as long as she'd let him.

She's mine—my tree siren.

"Olivia," he panted and chuckled. "You are driving me insane."

"I think we are both already insane," she said, sliding her hand up his chest and bopping him on the nose before standing there as he continued to lie under her.

"Come back," he pleaded, not liking the cold air between them, the front door still open. Olivia turned and looked outside, smiling.

"You want to put on a show?" he asked, trying to read her mind.

Olivia cocked her head and considered before kicking the door closed.

"I want to wrap myself inside a tree with you, so that no one else will ever see us again."

"I can see the appeal," Hunter said, sitting up, laughing at her boldness.

"Well, what are you waiting for?" Olivia demanded.

Hunter raised his eyebrows at her, a question in his eyes that Olivia only answered by pulling her jacket sleeve from her right arm. She then peeled it off slowly, not taking her eyes off of his. The mistletoe rose like a snake from the Garden of Eden, catching it as she let it drop.

"Great service here," Hunter joked, his smile disappearing entirely as he gulped, nerves hitting his stomach as the adrenaline high from their passionate makeout began to simmer down, because Olivia was just starting to heat up.

Her hand moved down to the waistband of her pants, which she unbuttoned, the tight fabric springing open to reveal black lace underwear. Hunter didn't need to remind himself where she got those, but damn, he was glad to see them on her.

Her pants were held up loosely by her hips, her exposed bikini line an open invitation for him to bury his head in between her thighs. He couldn't wait to see what she tasted like, what sounds escaped her perfect damn mouth.

He hoped she would giggle.

Fuck.

He nearly lost it then, blowing it all up just at the thought of his dark, powerful, terrifying woman falling apart from his tongue, a gentleness, a sweetness escaping through her shadowy facade.

He started to get to his feet, but Olivia wouldn't have it, using her foot to push his chest back down, his head bopping aggressively against the floor, pain flooding behind his eyes. There wasn't time to nurse himself, to let the ache subside, because Olivia was once again standing over him, and her pants were a little bit lower from her kick and now, he couldn't tear his attention away from how soft her skin looked, clean from the showers, healed from sleeping in his bed.

Thank God for that kick.

She was putting on a show, a moon shining bright for only him to see as she tugged on the bottom of her thick, brown, long-sleeved shirt, letting her hips sway back and forth, her long aphotic hair swaying behind her, voluminous, sticking to the wet parts of her mouth where his saliva still gleamed in the fragments of light navigating through the window and around the tall, out-of-control poinsettias that seemed intent on becoming their own jungle.

A moment later, the mistletoe rose again, catching the shirt that Olivia dropped to the floor, revealing a black lace bralette with no padding, her nipples pointed and pushing against the fabric just like his penis was still struggling against the constrictions of his pants.

Her torso was not long, not petite. She was so real. Someone who had been healing from pain, someone who sought comfort in his touch, someone whose body would soon be wrapped around his.

Hunter shook his head, and Olivia's face fell.

"Why is your face doing that?" she asked. "Do you not like my body?"

"Olivia." Hunter rushed up, his hands grabbing her hips, his fingers flexed around her ass. If he were any other man, he would bite her right there, sink his teeth into that soft, supple flesh, maybe even drawing blood. It would feel so good—she already felt so good. "You don't understand. I love everything about you. I have full devotion to your body."

He placed his mouth on her bikini line, a gentle kiss.

"I love right here, especially. I cannot stop staring at it. I am the luckiest man to be chosen to be wrapped up in a tree with you for all eternity."

Hunter pushed the little voice in the back of his head away, the one that told him that phrase wasn't a joke, it wasn't Olivia's twisted term of endearment. He was at her entrance, completely in benediction of the darling before him.

With his teeth, Hunter pulled the black lace cloth down just a bit, until the pants still hanging onto the shape of her upper thighs stopped him.

"Mmmmm," he groaned, seeing more skin and black curly hair like a vicious pillow, challenging him to come in, to get lower.

"No." Olivia pushed the palm of her hand against his forehead. "Now you go."

Hunter looked up at her, confused, before realization hit him.

He shuffled back away from her faster than he'd ever moved before, rivaling the speed of a shooting star, getting to his feet, standing so strong before Olivia, who sang songs of winter while the forest answered in blood.

Hunter's jacket, stained the haunting brown of the copper-smelling liquid, came off his shoulders and hit the floor. The mistletoe did not rise to give him the same service; there was no question of who the plant's favorite was.

Next was his shirt as he stood before her, smaller but still muscular arms, a small amount of curly chest hair to match the hair she had over her pelvis on display. There they were, feral animals, hurt and sitting in fear of their own, ready to comfort each other, ready to love each other.

"Set yourself free." Olivia raised a challenging eyebrow.

"Yes, Olivia," Hunter said, reaching down for the buckle, for the zipper, and letting the stretched fabric fly open. The extra space made him groan as his engorged penis jumped forward, still covered by his athletic gray boxers.

Olivia giggled and clapped, and the mistletoe writhed around her. One reaction happy, the other threatening.

Hunter wondered how much of that writhing botany was reacting to him, and how much was pulling from her subconscious.

"Are you sure?" Hunter asked. His hand rolled over his cock and his whole body tensed. Even if it was his touch, the excitement was from her teasing, even from looking at her ravishing body.

His eyes moved up from her hips to her belly button to her breasts, and then saw the gleam of the moon necklace. She held her shoulders back, presenting the token with pride, a prize, his prize.

Prize for what? You don't deserve her.

Hunter pushed the dark thought out of his mind, but it came back.

You heal your grief over Sarah by supporting death, by supporting murder. By reveling in it. By letting your cock get hard while there's blood on both of your faces.

Hunter gulped, nerves swirling.

There was no question that he wanted this, wanted her, wanted to entangle his limbs with hers forever, but he had spent so long wondering what Sarah would think of his life, if she would approve. She wouldn't approve of this.

He would have to move on completely. He couldn't look back.

This is who you have to be for her, Hunter reminded himself. *She needs you. You need her. She stepped out of the forest for you. You can step out of the shadow you live in for her.*

"Why are you taking so long?" Olivia pouted.

"I just want to make sure you want this," Hunter said, his fingers tapping against the waistband of his boxers. "I want to make sure it's not too quick, too fast."

"Hunter," Olivia whispered, her eyes sparkling and magical.

She opened her mouth, and the sweetest note came out of her throat, caressing around his heart, promising him safety and letting him know that not only did she want this, but she genuinely cared for him as well.

"That haze," Hunter murmured, "it's so hard to think clearly when it's there."

"I've waited one hundred years in a tree for someone to set me free, Hunter. I'm ready. I'm ready for you."

He closed his eyes and hummed like he'd had too many whiskeys.

You live in a fantasy now, Hunter. Embrace it.

Hunter opened his eyes, hungry, ready. Embrace it, he would.

The distance closed between them, Hunter finding Olivia's lips. It wasn't sweet, it wasn't gentle; the kiss was fire sizzling after being sprinkled with water, furious and roaring as his hands found her torso, traveling up to her breasts, squeezing as her own found the band of his boxers and let his cock out for air as she pulled down, both their heads and mouths following as she rounded her back to reach and stroke him.

"Mmmm," a deep guttural groan escaped his lips, and he pulled up for air. She was insatiable, unquenchable, and he ate up every flick of her wrist, every touch that started tender and then turned into a hard, pulsing grip.

Hunter got Olivia's panties lower and slid up her thighs with his length, feeling a slickness there already waiting for him.

He had had enough of his pep talks, of his internal dialogue, and would take what he wanted, what was being freely given, gifted. With that speed he'd found earlier, Hunter took Olivia's full ass in his hands and hiked her up, her legs wrapping around his torso as their lips found each other over and over again.

His feet moved back, stepping on mistletoe but ignoring the

sharp pain and the fresh blood he left on the floor before he walked into the hallway, hips, shoulders and elbows banging into the wooden walls as Olivia moaned and writhed on top of him, finding his dick in between her thighs right against her entrance.

They pushed through the doorway, entering his room as he threw her down on the bed. She squealed and smiled from the sudden playfulness, her legs hanging off the bed with her toes pointed. Hunter had been waiting for this. He was going to get so many answers as he stood between those pointed toes and moved down to his knees, grabbing her thighs and pulling her toward him.

21

CHAPTER TWENTY-ONE.

The dark green sheets clung to Olivia's skin like moss to bark, wrapping around her limbs as she twisted and arched beneath his weight. She reached for them instinctively, grabbing fistfuls of the bedding like she needed to hold on to something real. Her hands fisted near her ribs as her chest heaved, and she let out a sound—half gasp, half squeal—that went straight to his blood.

This was new. All of it.

Her.

Him.

Together.

And she bloomed.

Hunter knew she hadn't done this before—not like this, not with anyone who wanted her the way he did. Her every reaction was unfiltered, untrained, purely her. The way she trembled when he brushed his knuckles along the inside of her thigh, the way her breath hitched when his head dipped lower, the little strangled cry she made when his lips finally met the heat of her—those things undid him. Tore through his practiced self-control like it was paper.

He had thought he'd known desire. He hadn't known it like this.

Not how her fingers curled into his hair like vines desperate for an anchor.

Not the way she choked his name on a whimper when his tongue found the sensitive spot just above her entrance and began to work her open in slow, reverent circles.

Not her taste—both dark and bright, earthy and sweet. Like black coffee on the coldest morning. Like sap from a tree cracked open midwinter.

She was wildness and warmth, forest fire and frost.

And somehow, with his mouth pressed against her most vulnerable place, he felt safe.

Her hips bucked as she gasped again, louder this time, a sound full of shock and need. He anchored her with one arm across her belly, keeping her from floating away. His mouth never left her, tongue tracing patterns like he was writing a love letter she'd only feel, never read. And when he added the light swirl of his finger just beneath his lips, her body seized—a violent, beautiful quake.

She moaned like it was being dragged from her soul.

Hunter groaned into her, half-mad with how soft she was, how wet, how absolutely devastating it felt to know she was unraveling because of him. The way she tasted, it was endless. A cool, gushing stream across his tongue, salt and sweetness, and the coppery buzz of power humming beneath her skin. A sacred offering.

He wanted to drink from her forever.

He wanted to ruin her for anything else.

And he wanted her to know through every flick, every kiss, every whisper of teeth, this wasn't just hunger.

It was worship.

He pulled back just enough to look up at her.

Her eyes were half-lidded, dazed, and glowing in the lamplight. Her lips parted, chest rising and falling fast, her skin slick and shimmering as if the room had pulled the moon down to rest on her body. And when he reached up and kissed her inner thigh, softly this time, her hand shot out, fingers grasping blindly for him.

"H-Hunter ..." she stammered, the name a prayer, a plea, a tether.

He smiled, dark and tender, and kissed her again, higher this time.

"I'm right here," he murmured. "I'm not going anywhere."

"You better not," she sang out into the air between them, her face flushed with heat, proof of the fire she had just experienced. "I need more, Hunter. I demand more."

Hunter cocked his head and smiled. The timidity in her was gone, the innocence that he knew was there under a terrifying facade, gone. Here she was, his tree siren, the most powerful woman to ever exist, who took control of what she needed and wanted.

Even if it was nearly unbelievable, what she wanted was still him. Only him. And he would give his body and soul over to her indefinitely. She would consume him, and he would let her gladly.

Rising, his knees pushing against the edge of the bed, straddling Olivia, Hunter inched over her, not letting his body touch hers despite her protest.

He prolonged every moment, being able to look into her eyes again as his body planked over hers, fully nude, fully erect, just centimeters of space before it would nudge against her pelvis.

"Why are you waiting?" She pouted her bottom lip out. "I said more."

Hunter chuckled. "I wanted to hear it, I wanted to see it."

"See what?"

"You plead for me."

Olivia's pout changed instantly, recognizing the challenge that he was presenting her. She let out a high-pitched growl, her upper lip snarling as she grabbed his dick with her hand and gripped hard.

Hunter nearly yelped out as he pulled himself together; the shock of it almost had him spilling all over her, and he wasn't ready for this to be over. It was just getting started as far as he was concerned, and it would never end, not if he could help it.

He was feral for her touch, a wolf let out of his cage. The time for tension was gone, the time to make her plead and want was over as he pulled his hips back and his erection moved between her upper thighs until it hit tender flesh, until he could feel that slick wetness against his tip, her heat and her fire.

Olivia gasped as he pushed in, only an inch, his body in control despite the tight warmth that wrapped around him, that invitation to come in, to wrap himself inside of a tree to never again exit the forest.

"Are you okay?" He pulled himself back but was surprised when Olivia bolted up to her elbows, giggling.

That fucking giggle.

"Why did you stop?" she asked.

"The sound you made, I wanted to make sure I wasn't hurting you."

Olivia shook her head in disbelief, like looking at a sad, lost puppy begging for warm milk. "I gasped because you were so soft, so smooth. Much better than what I used to make out of the trees. Come inside me, Hunter. I want to feel you."

He didn't have any more will, any more restraint left after those words, after the encouragement to let himself go inside her. The last hour of foreplay, of kissing, of touching her, after consuming her had brought him here, a man ready to claim his reward.

She's no reward, you fool. You are beneath her.

He knew it; he accepted it, and he would do everything in his power to show his appreciation.

With a tilted, gentle push, Hunter had to stop his body from spasming as he entered Olivia, as her lips parted and air rushed out with a light, soft moan, a feminine praise.

"Fuck, Olivia." Hunter focused on the words, trying to desensitize himself, "You feel incredible. Indescribable."

Her tender flesh hugged him, the perfect opening that treated him as if he were the king, as if it were her that was worshiping him.

Stay focused on her.

Hunter kissed Olivia's neck, moving down, sucking gently as he moved delicately, finding every angle possible to hit inside her, the head of his cock leading the charge to victory, to her ultimate pleasure.

Control yourself, Hunter.

It was becoming impossible, impossible to contain himself so that he could focus only on her, but he was determined. That was until Olivia decided to take control, to hold his balls in her very hands as she wrapped her legs around his torso and violently rolled to the right. Hunter was quickly on his back with her mounted on top of him, her face up toward the ceiling, her hair wild, tangled, cascading down her shoulders and back as her hips moved forward and back rhythmically as if she were riding a horse.

You're a damn lucky horse.

"I'm almost there, Hunter," she moaned, her fingertips brushing her navel and traveling up her breasts, up her neck, finding her lips, her mouth, as she sucked and moaned as she rode him harder and harder.

"I'm not going to make it," Hunter yelled. "Not when you move like that."

His whole body was moments from seizing. She was a force, her movements something he had never had before. He grabbed onto her hips with force, pulling her forward, not letting her roll back, trying to stay with her, trying to make sure that she didn't get left behind at that moment.

But the way his cock twitched inside her, the way her slit slid against his pelvis when he grabbed, must have been the stars, the moon, that she had been looking for, praying for, because in that moment Olivia arched back, her pussy so tight, her thighs shaking against the side of his as she pulled every muscle in. Her head fell back, and she let out a howl, a musical note that promised all things macabre, a deathly sexual release that reached all things spirits and wind and trees.

Hunter let himself go too, and the room started spinning as he spilled into her, as he gave all of himself to her. She now had some of him inside of her forever to keep, forever to manipulate, forever to obey, and he would gladly do it all over and over again.

As their panting and gasps were still at a high, a wave of shock flooded through Hunter, because for the first time ever, his orgasm was responded to with a force, with destruction and horror.

An explosive roar burst out, a monster, a dragon, there to scream into Hunter's ears, and he wondered if he would ever hear a normal sound again. Protectively, he flung himself up and around Olivia, tossing them both off the side of the bed, thudding against the floor as he shook over her from adrenaline, among other things.

The house trembled, and broken glass joined the symphony of destruction as the perfect percussionist. Hunter just listened, still holding her, not moving as his body started to feel the impact of their tumble down. He was sore, with a huge ache in his neck that he hoped was not an injury.

After the commotion calmed, Hunter blinked and looked into Olivia's eyes with panic, a sudden reminder that a person was wrapped in his arms. He pulled back, looking into her pupils. No dissociation, just that mischievous smile, that eyebrow raise.

He was human, so it seemed the only appropriate thing to ask, despite that look she gave him: "Are you okay?"

Olivia broke out into a full laugh, so melodic and filled with beauty, with joy. She clapped her hands together and lifted her chin to look over the bed.

"Did you see what we did?" she asked him. "Did you see what you did?"

What I did?

"Every moment I'm with you," Olivia continued, "is confirmation that the right person sang for me."

Hunter carefully got to his feet and stood. Olivia watched him rise, his queen on her knees before him. His cock twitched as the thought flashed through his mind. It disappeared quickly, which was very unfortunate for him, as he now had something new to look forward to, to feel her mouth, her tongue, with his full length pushing toward her throat.

Instead, he saw what had happened—the monstrous noise that brought chaos and destruction—just on the opposite side of the bed. He had been right to roll the way he did, because if he had chosen the other way, they might not have made it.

The walls and windows of his room were destroyed, completely pushed down in half as bricks lay loose like debris after a bombing. It was no dragon, no monster; the cause was something entirely too familiar but also unrecognizable.

Hunter stared at the tree in his front yard after it had fallen violently into his home, bringing coldness and darkness with it. Olivia beamed, proud, as if there were no greater accomplishment.

22

CHAPTER TWENTY-TWO.

The warmest, most welcoming colors filled the room. Reds like heirloom tomatoes, yellows that tried to disguise themselves as gold, and oranges that tasted like autumn cascaded over his carpet, the edge of his bed, and into his closet and hallway.

"Is that my tree? From my front lawn?" Hunter blinked at it, knowing that it was the only explanation. The sugar maple for which he had spent so much time destroying the television for was smaller, its leaves bare from the throes of winter. This seemed like an entirely different tree that was thriving in the early autumn.

"Isn't she beautiful?" Olivia beamed, a naked beacon of wildness.

"She?"

"What else did you expect?"

Hunter sighed, "I don't know how to clean this up."

"Why clean it up? The tree is perfectly happy here."

The sound of doors slamming caught Hunter's attention as he heard gasps and footsteps approaching.

"Oh my God, I hope no one got hurt."

"Herb, call the paramedics just in case."

"Knock on the door—what if they need help?"

The neighbors.

The sound of the tree falling, of crashing through roof, wall, and window, must have woken up quite a few people.

Hunter tripped over branches, wincing as he stepped on small, sharp-edged sticks hidden by leaves. He rushed to his closet to try to recover any clothing that would cover them both before they flashed the entire neighborhood. The horrifying picture of paramedics forcing them both to sit on a gurney, strapped, nude, played on the screen of his mind.

Fuck. Fuck. Fuck.

"Hello?" Hunter heard an elderly voice croak. "It's your neighbor Ethel in nineteen-nineteen. A tree fell on your house."

No shit, lady.

"Are you alright? My husband is calling the paramedics."

Ethel was yelling so loudly that Hunter was sure the entire neighborhood would be gathering there, if they were not already.

"We are okay, please don't call for help," Hunter shouted, throwing a t-shirt and boxers at Olivia. "Put those on."

"You would prefer this on me?" she challenged, an eyebrow raised and an amused expression on her lips.

Hunter sighed, letting the dark win his internal game of tug of war again.

"If I had it my way," Hunter growled, "you would never wear clothes again around me."

"I would prefer it that way, too." Olivia smiled. "The trees, they agree obviously."

Hunter poked his head through the wet t-shirt, which he was able to pull and rip from under a different branch.

"Obviously? Nothing is obvious to me about these trees."

Olivia's smile faltered, but Hunter's stress started to subside when she matched his actions by putting on the clothes.

"Hello!" Ethel's voice yelled. "HELP. IS. ON. THE. WAY. STAY. CALM. Oh my God, Madge, is that you? That poor widower might be dead in there."

"Did you see the containment on Main Street?" Hunter assumed he was hearing Madge now. "People are saying it was terrorists."

"George, don't we have his mother's phone number? She comes to church sometimes. An awful, posh woman."

"Do not call my mom!" Hunter yelled.

"Did you hear that?" One of them said excitedly. Probably Ethel. "Someone's alive!"

Hunter heard probably Ethel dramatically clear her throat. "DO. NOT. MOVE. HELP. IS. COMING."

"Should we go inside?"

"God no, who knows how gruesome a scene it could be. I wouldn't be able to sleep for weeks with gore in my mind."

Right on cue, the faint sound of sirens reached his ears, and it seemed to be all that was needed to get the parade of retirees to shut up.

You'll need to get used to that—the sound of sirens.

"I think they'll be disappointed that you survived," Olivia said, stepping over branches and leaves barefoot as if she were merely walking on soft clouds. As soon as she reached him, she dove into his arms, nearly knocking him back into the split wall of the hallway.

"Can you see it, Hunter?" Olivia looked at the leaves, caressing what she could touch in the palm of her hand without breaking their body contact. "Can you see what our love has grown? It's so lovely; these colors are more vibrant than the forest before the leaves frost."

"Love?" He got tongue-tied on the word.

"When our bodies, when our souls connected," she replied as if it were the easiest thing in the world.

"Why did the tree fall into the house, Olivia?" Hunter asked.

The sirens were growing louder. Ethel and Madge had started gossiping again, though they were no longer yelling.

"You took me away from my body in a way that I can never let go of," she said. "The tree grew, its flowers bloomed, as I did."

"Right," said Hunter, turning Olivia around so that she faced him. "We should walk out front. I expect this is quite a scene."

Scenes seemed to follow Olivia around. It was just another part of his role as Olivia's new lover, as her devoted, to cover and shield her from the mundaneness of their world's laws and ordinances.

Love.

Everything seemed new, all rugs pulled up from underneath him, a stumbling fawn too easily entrapped in the thick vines of the wood, vulnerable and unprotected.

But who did he need protection from? The very person he was trying to protect?

The two stepped out of the opening in the wall and walked into the living room, out the front door. The sky had begun to lighten, the promise of daylight welcoming the firetruck that took up the entire street as it blasted its sirens and lights, another circus for their town to gossip about.

Hunter was in a daze. His vision was blurred enough for him to realize that he had stayed up the entire night, that his body was exhausted, and that his nervous system was slightly in shock. He gripped Olivia's hand, his new comfort item, as a firefighter walked up to them, standing outside the front door.

Hunter saw the man's lips move, but he heard no sound, as if the world had been put on mute. He was aware enough to know that Olivia spoke to the firefighter, that her face lit up with a smile, and that she pointed toward the tree.

What was she saying to him?

"Sir, sir?" The firefighter snapped his fingers a few times in front of his face, getting Hunter's attention. Then, as the world became unbearably loud, the firefighter turned the volume back up.

"You're bleeding, sir. The back of your head got scraped up pretty bad. Let me take a look at it."

Hunter was stunned. He didn't remember getting hit by anything.

"He jumped over me to shield me," Olivia said, staring up at him, her protector.

"That's admirable," the fireman said. "Honestly, this entire situation is crazy. The dirt around the roots is so soft, as if they somehow wanted to come up on their own."

"It's almost like the tree wanted to come inside." Olivia gave a sweet smile as the fireman took Hunter's arm and sat him down on the ground. More of his colleagues swarmed, testing his vision with lights, checking for a concussion, and bandaging his head.

"I think I just need some sleep," Hunter said, trying to shoo away the help.

The sound of a car driving up and slamming its brakes caught Hunter's attention. The violent, panicked slam of a car door was followed by gasps.

"Hi, Mom." Hunter sighed.

23

CHAPTER TWENTY-THREE.

unter's mom was always a force to be reckoned with, but watching her in a state of emergency was an entirely new matter.

"Why would a tree just fall over, that seems like incredibly poor city planning to allow such large trees to be planted within such a small lot," she said throwing her hands into the air as she marched back and forth in Hunter's living room while he stared at her from the couch, Olivia leaning heavily into his side.

The paramedics had come and gone after they got a piece of her mind, and the firefighters had reluctantly taken off as well. After lots of yelling, the parade of neighbors who stood in their driveways pretending to be good, concerned citizens, also departed.

"I'm an adult," Hunter reminded Minerva. "You didn't need to interfere."

"Nonsense, Hunter. You have a supportive family. I urge you to be more grateful for that. Where can I find your collection of tote bags?"

"I can't say that I collect them."

"Well, what else would you pack some things in?"

"A suitcase?" Hunter suggested.

Minerva threw her hands up in the air again. "Well, let's get that. We need to pack for a few nights, though it'd be better to plan through New Year's at least."

"And where is it that we are packing for?"

"My house, of course. You cannot stay here. Do you know how to contact your homeowner's insurance? We will want to do that right away."

Hunter stood. "No need. We can stay here. The bathroom and kitchen are intact."

Minerva wasn't hearing it, though, and stomped off towards the hallway. Hunter stared at Olivia, who smiled as they listened to his mom wrestle with leaves and branches, rustling, snapping, and polite curses audible in the not-too-distant background.

"What is she doing?" Hunter pinched the bridge of his nose.

"I think it's sweet how much she cares about you," Olivia said. "You should let people take care of you, Hunter."

"Why is that?"

"Because it's often not about you at all. They offer for reasons that are often entirely self-serving. Don't deny her something that she so desperately needs."

Hunter thought about it, and maybe Olivia was right. He didn't go back to the forest because he was worried about Olivia. Initially, he'd gone back because he couldn't handle his conscience, the guilt of never knowing what might have happened to her. His mom had been overbearing the moment he moved out, needing to be involved in every detail, from planning his wedding to Sarah to even helping them buy this house.

"You could be right," Hunter said.

Maybe Mom needed this.

"Right then, it looks like we get to spend Christmas together." Minerva popped back in, holding a suitcase that looked stuffed to the brim and one of the bags of clothes that she had just bought for Olivia.

"I'm convinced that you hadn't put all of this away yet," she said, beaming as the shiny rectangular bag swayed in her hand. She moved over to the kitchen and began sorting through a stack of papers on the counter, separating them into piles.

"Mom, you've got to stop," Hunter rolled his eyes.

"Nonsense," she said, putting one of the stacks into the top zipper pocket of the carry-on-sized suitcase. "I'm your mom—this is my job. Now come on, we may be able to make it back before your father drinks all the coffee I brewed this morning. You both look like you could use a shower and a nap. Chop chop!"

Hunter held his hand out to Olivia, and she stood up.

"Yes, sleep would be great," Hunter said, his head throbbing.

"By the way, don't think I haven't noticed how much effort you've put into the holiday plants I left last time. Olivia, you must have a seriously green thumb," Minvera said, marching towards the front door.

"I suppose." Olivia smiled, following, pulling Hunter behind her.

THIRTY MINUTES LATER, Hunter found himself in the backseat of his mom's car, the white leather smelling like it had recently been detailed. They had pulled into the long driveway of his childhood home.

"You haven't come home in so long." Minerva sighed with relief. "To have this house filled with some life again is so needed."

It was true. He hadn't been back since Sarah died. Closing

himself off in his modest home for such a long time had made him really see the opulence in which he'd grown up. The lot in itself was at least an acre. No neighbors packed in, everyone in the neighborhood was certainly too occupied with their own success to be nosy, to even notice if something was off in their community.

They drove through a gate made of thin black metal rods supported by brick pillars, their family name plated in gold and molded onto the face of the left brick post.

Trimmed hedges frosted with ice lined the way up the rest of the driveway, showing them the way until his mom pulled up to the multistory lilac-colored home with large white support beams framing the entrance to the home. A detached garage sat beside them, along with his father's black Toyota Tacoma.

"Welcome to the Gunnan family compound," his mom trilled, turning off the sedan and opening her door. "Oh, I wonder if it's too late to have the caterer bring a holiday ham now that we have the extra people. Now, don't worry about gifts. You've been through a lot, and I'll make sure that everyone has items to unwrap."

"Gifts?" Olivia repeated, confused.

"Tomorrow is Christmas Eve, dear," Minerva said. "Come on now, Hunter, your father will be happy to see you."

He moved out of the backseat and up to Olivia's door, opening it for her. If his mom saw her opening her own door, he imagined that he would get an earful later.

"What do you think?" Hunter asked her as she blinked at him from her seat. He leaned over her lap, his hand sliding up her thigh and her hot breath against his neck. He reached down until she heard a click, his hand pushing down to let her seatbelt free.

"Let's go, kids," Minerva shouted behind her, her heeled boots stomping on the stone-paved path covered in salt. "You can kiss later."

"Don't mind if I do," Hunter whispered, letting his lips find Olivia's in a swift, sweet moment.

Minerva stood waiting for them up the three steps leading to the home's entrance, large potted plants scattered around the edge catching Olivia's eye.

"Nice to see that you're still a gentleman," Hunter's mom said before turning and opening the double doors into the home. "This house, Olivia, has been in my family for a few generations now. One day it'll belong to Hunter, and then his children. I'm assuming there will be many."

This was it; this was when he murdered his poor, overeager mom.

"Not presumptuous at all, Mom," Hunter said through his teeth.

"What do you think?" Minerva asked, completely ignoring Hunter. She pulled Olivia's attention away from the plants by grabbing her arm and dragging her inside.

"About what?" Olivia asked, staring up at the open vaulted ceiling, the banister railing, and the elegant staircase that greeted them.

"Well, about children, of course," Minerva laughed, taking her coat off and hanging it on the rack in the entryway.

"I was a child before," Olivia said.

Hunter had to turn his head over his shoulder to prevent his mom from seeing him laugh. He grunted a few times.

"Excuse me, something in my throat."

"Hmmm," Minerva said, displeased.

"Honestly, Mom, I feel like I might fall over at any minute. What room should we use? We need some rest."

"You're not even going to say hello to your father?" Minerva scoffed. "Mark, Hunter, and his ... friend ... are here. I picked them up because a tree fell on his house."

"I'm about to step in the shower, welcome," Mark shouted back from somewhere upstairs, a door closing.

"Well, I guess that's that," Hunter said. "What room?"

Minerva sighed. "Second on the right upstairs."

"Thanks, Mom," Hunter said, kissing her on the cheek. "I appreciate everything you're doing for us."

He had to give it to her. She was killing herself from the excitement of him being here, and his words worked—she seemed to perk right back up.

"Go rest. When you two come back down, I'll make sure there is a bounty of food. I'll have your father grab your bags and put them by your door when he's ready for the day."

Taking Olivia's hand, Hunter led the two of them upstairs. The soft beige carpet melted under their feet, and the walls were lined with acrylic paintings of oranges and limes. He entered the room that was once his childhood bedroom, now turned into a posh guest room with purple bedding and seasonal winter flowers sitting atop a dresser in the corner.

"She can be a lot," Hunter apologized.

"Your mother? How lovely it must be to have a mother."

Hunter put his arms around Olivia, and the two fell into bed, closing their eyes while wrapped around one another.

24

CHAPTER TWENTY-FOUR.

When the light fell away and the room darkened, Hunter and Olivia finally stirred. Hunter lay there, staring at her face, her eyelashes, as she slowly woke up before him, a doll turning into life.

"Hi." He smiled, and his heart skipped a beat when she smiled back. Olivia put her hand on the back of his neck, pulling his face into hers as they shared a sweet kiss, their lips parting slowly, savoring the moment.

"How could we stay like this forever?" Hunter mused.

"I can think of a way," Olivia teased, allowing Hunter to move in for another kiss, and then another, and another as his hands slid down to her thighs.

Knock. Knock. Knock.

"Hunter, Hunter, are you awake yet?" His mom's voice came through the door. "You left your phone in the car. Your father brought it in, and it has been nonstop pinging all day. I checked it because it felt like an emergency, and well, I think you should look at it."

Fucking hell.

"I called your homeowner's insurance for you. They're sending someone out on the twenty-sixth. You're welcome," Minerva said from the door.

Hunter sighed, got off the bed, and went to the door. Minerva stood there, holding his phone out to him as he opened it.

"Thanks, Mom," he said.

"When are you coming downstairs?"

Hunter checked his phone, seeing his co-worker group text had gone wild that day. His mom watched him like a hawk as he read through it.

SADIE 8:23 AM:

Who even has a funeral on Christmas Eve?
How tragic.

CELIA 8:25 AM:

You know we all have to go. We were there.

ELAINE 8:26 AM:

I think it sounds beautiful, in a dark, sordid
way.

NINA 8:29 AM:

I'm still in this group chat.

DARIUS 8:32 AM:

Oops. Well, I'm coming to the funeral, Nina.
I'm sorry for your loss.

Hunter exited the group chat and scrolled to his email, where there was a formal invitation awaiting him for Tom's funeral tomorrow at eleven in the morning.

"Tom ... died." Hunter turned towards Olivia. "The night we were at the market, Tom died."

Poor Nina.

His mom put her hand to her heart.

"You poor thing, you've been through such an ordeal. I'll see you downstairs for dinner."

Hunter closed the door as his mom walked away.

"There is a funeral tomorrow," he said. "We should go."

"I'm sorry, Hunter. I'm sorry if I killed your friend." She took his face in her hands.

Hunter nodded, appreciative of her apology.

This is who you are now, Hunter. She will kill, and you agreed to protect her.

The light side in his internal tug of war was suddenly winning the battle as guilt began to creep inside him, gasoline directly from the pump, just waiting for a match to fall. He was raised, as most were, to be good, to be kind, not to take any lives.

She isn't evil, he told himself. *She's heartbroken. She's been alone.*

It was hard for Hunter to see someone who rose up from hell. Instead, he saw a wounded puppy who needed love and would give it in return.

You need love, too.

"Would you like to take a shower? My parents are expecting us downstairs."

"Will you join me?" Olivia asked.

Hunter's sorrowful look was nearly instantly eradicated as he opened the bedroom door, his arm pointing out. "After you."

Her hand grazed his pelvis, a tickle, as she walked through.

AN HOUR LATER, fully recovered and impeccably cleaned, the

couple sat down at the table in the formal dining room, plates of mashed potatoes and halibut in front of them.

Hunter's dad, Mark, sat across from Hunter, taking slow bites of his meal with large gulps of red wine, slowly draining the glass.

"Your friend's dead then?" his dad asked, breaking the silence. "A bit fast to get the body back, but I suppose if it's just cremation then—"

"Not appropriate dinner conversation, Mark," his mom cut in, too bubbly. "How about instead, Olivia, tell me what is it that you do, or want to do?"

"What I do?" Olivia questioned, poking the fish.

"Olivia loves plants, gardening, trees," Hunter chimed in.

"Really?" Mark's interest piqued.

"Will you open a nursery, then?" Minerva asked. "I think it would be grand to own a nursery. You could hire people to work for you and visit whenever you'd like to see your hard work."

Olivia shook her head. "I do not want to be around people. I try, for Hunter, but it is not my preference."

Minerva seemed like she could not comprehend the thought; she'd always been entirely too social.

"I understand that," Mark chimed in.

"So then what, get married and be a housewife?"

"Why would I want to do that either?" Olivia asked.

"What else is there?" Minerva asked, eyebrows almost defeating the Botox to rise.

"The forest—" Olivia started to say, but Hunter cut her off.

"Olivia is on furlough, trying to decide what direction she wants to take."

"Oh, how lovely," Minerva said, "to have that opportunity to explore. Isn't it lovely, Mark?" Hunter's father grunted and nodded his head. "I just mean that a woman who wants an exploratory life needs to marry into money. And until we both die, Hunter has none."

"Mom." Hunter stared. "We will be attending a funeral tomorrow morning. The timing isn't ideal—I know how important the holidays are to you—but we should really be there to support."

"Oh yes, well, you'll have to go to that by yourself. Olivia and I have plans," his mom responded while pushing her food around on her plate.

Hunter looked at Olivia, who just shrugged at him.

"I'm sorry, what plans do you two have?"

"Well, I have to take Olivia shopping for the ball at the manor tomorrow night."

"I didn't realize we were all going to that." Hunter raised his eyebrows, not excited at all to dance formally at the place where he had gotten married.

"We are not all going," Minerva said with obvious frustration. "The two of you are. I packed an envelope with the tickets from your kitchen counter."

Hunter wracked his mind, not putting together what she was saying, but finally, the memory hit him.

The teachers' raffle prize.

"I can't imagine you would deny Olivia a chance to be twirled around to a small orchestra on Christmas Eve. I couldn't imagine something so romantic. I know exactly where to take you for your gown. Hunter, there's a tux in your father's closet that will fit you fine."

Hunter looked at Olivia, a new ping of guilt building in his chest. He hadn't even thought of the ball or inviting her. How very like Minerva to instigate this situation.

"Is it the manor by the forest?" Olivia asked him.

Hunter nodded.

"Home," Olivia said.

"Home?" Minerva questioned.

"Home," Olivia confirmed with no context.

"You're quite strange, aren't you, Olivia?" Mark laughed. "We could use some of that energy around here."

Hunter reached his hand out and put it on top of Olivia's. "We can go."

The dark-haired beauty before him smiled sweetly, looking down into her lap. She looked so out of place in the quiet opulence of the room they were in, with the crown molding up above them and the napkin rings gleaming silver from the low, yellow light bulbs glowing from shaded vintage lamps. Olivia was born into a world of wealth and yet did not seem at all at home when surrounded by it.

There were no plants in this room, Hunter realized, with the exception of the fresh thyme sprinkled over his plate. Surely, Olivia had noticed, too. Perhaps that's why she looked so out of place here. Hunter didn't like it; he didn't like seeing her sitting there, a product for his mom to create, a future perfect wife.

That wasn't Olivia. He didn't want that for her. He wouldn't accept that for her.

Inheriting his family home felt ever further away, a possibility that he could spit on, unless Olivia could make trees run through the windows and intertwine themselves in the walls, a ghostly version of the picture-perfect life the estate did its best to emulate.

Olivia wanted the forest. And Hunter wanted Olivia.

"I'll take you, of course," Hunter said. "We can go tomorrow night. My mom's right, you should get a dress."

Bringing Tom's murderer to his funeral, on second thought, would be looked down upon. If Olivia existed, who was to say that angels were not looking down on them right then? It seemed better not to test the theory, not until he felt like the two of them were safe, not until he was sure they had forever in the palms of their hands with fists closing.

"We are going to have the best time." Minerva put down her wineglass, absolutely giddy. "And after the ball—the tickets said it ended at midnight—you'll come here for a night of sleep. When you wake, we will have a traditional Christmas. The caterer did not mind accounting for the extra people at all. In the evening, your aunt will be coming with the rest of her family. All those children, she is a breeder. We come from good genes, what a blessing."

"What do you do?" Olivia asked.

Minerva blinked at her, as if it were the silliest question in the world.

"Well, dear, I am a housewife. I raised a child and took care of the estate."

"That sounds lonely. I know how that feels, to be lonely." Olivia said.

"Well, dinner was lovely," Mark said. "I'm all finished. Will we be playing cards in the living room tonight? Your mother loves that."

Hunter looked at his mom. Her eye almost twitched as she tried to avoid Olivia's stare.

"You know, tomorrow is a big day," his mom said, pushing her plate away from her. "I'd rather get some rest. Thank you for coming down to dinner. I know it's been a hard day for you with the tree and your home."

Minerva stood up and exited the room.

Mark cleared his throat while Hunter took Olivia's hand under the table.

"She thought she'd lost you after Sarah, son. You're starting to come back to life. I know Olivia here is to thank you for that. You know that she's trying—she's trying so hard to make Olivia feel welcome. I can tell that she will be a part of your life for a long time."

Hunter looked over toward Olivia. "If she wants me, I'll be there."

Olivia smiled.

"I want you, but I don't want this," she said.

I know.

Mark frowned, his hands out, gesturing toward the rest of the house. "You're well suited for each other, then. Hunter doesn't want this either."

"I know," she replied, "isn't he perfect?"

25

____

CHAPTER TWENTY-FIVE.

Without Olivia by his side, Hunter felt like he was missing a limb. At least that was how it seemed as he stepped up to the church the next morning. He was alone with a clear blue sky, the sun shining with a vengeance despite the temperature plummeting more than in the previous few days. When the gray and the clouds departed, it was always colder. There was a strange comfort in the claustrophobic press of the storm. The haunting, stormy skies wrapped around him like a blanket, holding in the warmth—just like the phantom ache of his missing limb.

Just like Olivia.

Hunter stood there on the walkway, and the tan brick structure's gothic, tall, pointed architecture didn't feel welcoming at all. Inside, he knew, would be his coworkers, and a person who'd been killed at the hands of the person he loved.

Loved.

You fucking love her.

Of course, he did. He wouldn't be here, he wouldn't be protecting her from what she did, if he didn't. She was no monster. She was his.

My moon. My tree siren.

It's time, Sarah. It's time to move on.

Tears started accumulating in Hunter's eyes, a few droplets falling and staining his white button-up shirt and black tie.

"No shame, man." Darius walked up behind him, slapping his shoulders. "I didn't care about Tom, but I don't think I'll be able to get through this without crying either."

"Saying goodbye, closing a door for good, is the hardest thing I've ever done," Hunter admitted, nodding his head. "But I love Olivia. I can't believe I'd ever say that again."

"We are talking about two different people," Darius said. "But congratulations, I'm happy for you. I could see you disappearing, wrapped in love, never to be seen again."

"That would kill my mom."

"Kill, what a word to use here," said Sadie, walking up behind them. "Let's get this over with, shall we? I think the rest of our group is already inside."

A few other people dressed in black walked around the three of them, entering the church. Hunter, Darius, and Sadie walked in behind them, entering a large room with wooden pews, a closed coffin surrounded by flowers at the front. He had been here before. He had done this before. His chest slowly rose and fell as he was hurled towards a pew in the middle of the room.

Before he sat down, he spotted a grieving Nina in the front row, her body shaking as she wiped her tears from her face. He knew this. He had been through this.

I'm sorry, Nina.

Hunter sat between Darius and Nina, noticing Elaine and Celia a few spots down. Both of them looked entirely too fabulous with bold red lips and dark glasses, even indoors.

He was stuck—caught between two worlds, and two versions of himself. One was the man who had known a normal life, who had loved Sarah too deeply and mourned her for years. The other lived in a new reality, one shaped by the woman who made him think of the moon, who made darkness feel like the very source of beauty and power.

He could never see the night the same way again. His entire worldview had shifted, and there was no going back.

How do you move forward? How do you wrap yourself in that darkness? In her world of trees and stars?

"Thank you, thank you for coming to honor our departed beloved, Tom." A minister moved toward the casket, a microphone on his lapel.

A large sob erupted from Nina.

Everyone who could reach put their arms on her for comfort.

He hated how sadness permitted people to touch you. He'd never understood why that was a comfort. That was why he'd quickly disappeared into his house, into his hobbies. He couldn't stand the compassionate touch on the shoulder, the arms out wide embrace offered, but felt like he had to accept it.

I won't touch you, Nina, he promised her, though she would never hear it. *I will leave you be so you can find your own way. So you won't be confused.*

Hunter, on the other hand, was finding so much clarity in those moments of collective grief. The support given was so wrong. He gripped his hands into fists, sitting there through the rest of the funeral, through the strangers who stood on the stage, saying their public goodbyes and giving the families their condolences.

It was such a show.

This just cannot be how you say goodbye.

For the rest of his time there, Hunter only dreamed of the night sky, of the shine of the stars that reminded him of Olivia's hair, the awkwardness of her words that brought so much clarity to him, her social graces gone from her time away from humans, from ceremony.

That woman was so strong. She knew what she wanted, and even though it was absolutely terrifying, she went for it. People got hurt in the process, and perhaps they always would.

Hunter shook his head and chuckled to himself. The naked woman in the forest, the one that needed his help, the damsel, was anything but. She was so complex that now he had no choice but to rethink his entire life, all of his choices.

I can't wait to get back to you.

As sniffles and tears flowed through the gathering, Hunter's mind wandered to her. This was a funeral for Tom, yes, but it felt like more than that, a funeral for who he was once, a door closed on the chapter that he had been working these past few days to leave behind.

Poetic, that thought, with bodies cold in their caskets.

So was the person that Hunter once was. That person had loved so differently, needed so differently. The person who hadn't been an individual, but a part of a marriage. He'd been no one outside of that.

Now he was different. Now, he had a job to protect and to love Olivia.

It was a job he couldn't abandon—no matter how bloody it might get.

Sarah had shown him obsession, but Olivia had taught him how to love so imperfectly, filled with mess and iron and mischievousness. She showed him to love with his soul, not his brain.

She was with his mother right now, being dressed to look like someone else's doll. She was no doll, but the moon, the stars, the crimson red of blood against pine.

Dread and anxiousness filled him, a macabre sense that told him to run, to get out of this place filled with someone else's loss—that he had a full life to live with the woman who had wrapped herself around his heart, his bones, his organs.

Never before has there been more beauty in my life, he thought to himself as the crowd rose, as bodies around him hugged one another in comfort. They all moved to the front of the church, forming a line of dread and mourning, white flowers with large petals coercing their hearts towards the dead body that they were all there to say goodbye to.

I have to get her out of here.

The realization dawned on him.

Darius pushed Hunter out of the pew and into the line.

Olivia couldn't be here.

She couldn't be in this town.

She couldn't build a life where she knew nothing, where everything was foreign to her. She would never have peace if she were always a danger to people.

If Olivia wanted to rot in a forest, Hunter would support that dream. He would be damn sure to make it happen.

My girl. My tree siren.

"It was a beautiful ceremony," Darius said as he pushed past Hunter. They made it to the front of the line, and his coworkers began hugging Nina, who couldn't even look them in the eye. She looked like she wanted to jump out of her skin, like this was a complete nightmare for her, being here at this church surrounded by this sympathy.

I know, Nina, I've been there. I won't touch you.

"I'm sorry," Hunter said to her. "I know how much it hurts. Even now, I still feel it."

Nina looked up to him, blinking, realizing, remembering that he had once been right where she stood. Her bottom lip trembled.

"The last conversation we had was about a gingerbread house competition," she said.

"It doesn't matter, Nina," Hunter tried. "What matters is that he did it with you, even though he probably didn't want to."

"You are terrible at this," Sadie said through clenched teeth.

"No, no," Nina said, "You're right. He hated those things."

"But he still did them. He did them for you," Hunter said. "You were the love of his life. You made his life worth living. You did that, Nina. You gave him it all."

"Okay, a little better now," Sadie whispered.

Nina nodded as Celia went in for a hug, Elaine embracing them both as the church emptied.

"Merry Christmas," Nina said, pushing the group away. She needed to be alone now, Hunter remembered. Hunter was still not quite past that, always preferring to be alone.

Until Olivia.

"Merry Christmas," Hunter said. "I've got to go."

"Where are you running off to?" Sadie asked, following him as he turned and walked down the aisle.

"I've got a ball to attend."

"You're actually going to that? And you're not taking me?"

"Blame my mother."

~

An hour had passed, the sun having moved to the western skies. His mother's car was not in the driveway, so they were still gone. Hunter heard a small commotion when he stepped out onto the cement: the sound of metal falling and clanging, followed by a muffled swear.

"Dad," Hunter yelled out, walking towards the garage, passing his dad's truck. "Is that you I hear?"

His dad popped his head out, his handsome full head of salt and pepper hair, dirt on his cheeks, grimy yellow gloves on his hands.

"Ah, Hunter, you're back. Come help me with this."

He walked over, turning the corner to see inside the garage door, and stopped to laugh at its absurdity.

"Dad, what are you doing with a motorcycle?"

"It's been my little project," Mark said, picking up a wrench from a gigantic red toolbox. "I've been teaching myself how to fix it. It's nearly there. I'm replacing the brake pads today."

"Can't say that I can actually help. This is one hobby I never got into."

"You're alright; why don't you just keep me company? Your mother doesn't care for this, so it's usually just me out here by myself. How was the funeral?"

Hunter picked at some tools on a basic wooden cabinet. "I said goodbye."

"Ah, but not to the recently deceased, I assume."

Hunter turned, looking at his father in surprise. "What do you mean?"

"I know you, son. I don't know much about this Olivia girl, but I know that your heart is now hers. I also know that she doesn't belong here."

"Doesn't belong here?"

His father couldn't know.

Could he?

"I can't say I know where it is that she does belong, but she sticks out clearly," Mark said. "That can't be a surprise to you, can it? You can't keep something caged where it doesn't belong."

"That something being Olivia?"

Mark nodded, going back to his bike. Hunter listened to him grunt and curse under his breath for a few minutes.

"You think we should leave?" Hunter eventually asked.

"No, son," Mark said. "I just know that you will. Hell, I probably would, too. There is a lot of pain here for you. I don't know how you did it, living in that same house for all that time."

"Mom would miss me too much." Hunter rubbed the back of his head.

"I think it would be better for her."

"Better? Would it be better for me to leave?"

"It would be better for you to leave than to keep watching

your soul die slowly. You never recovered; you never reinvented your life. It was hard to watch."

Hunter shook his head, anger building slowly, smoke rising in a hay barrel. "I'm sorry that my grief affected you all so terribly."

Mark sighed. "I've never needed to be a poet, Hunter. I've never needed to be great with words in my line of work. Direct has always been best."

"Just say it, Dad. Whatever it is, please say it so I can continue to hide in the house."

"I'll have to follow you in there. Your mother insists we figure out which suit of mine fits you best."

Mark got up from the motorcycle and started peeling off his gloves, setting them on top of the toolbox.

"Did you finish those brake pads?" Hunter asked.

"Of course not, I have no idea what I'm doing."

Hunter laughed.

"Son." Mark walked up to him, throwing his arm around Hunter's shoulder. The touch was awkward; their family was not affectionate in this way, especially not his dad. Mark usually wrote checks that Hunter refused to cash.

The two walked out of the garage, the sun at their backs.

Why aren't they back yet?

"I just need you to know," Mark continued, "that it doesn't matter what you do with your life. No matter what, I support it. I trust that you know what's best for you."

The words sank deep. Hunter was surprised at how much the sentiment meant to him. Acceptance and approval were not normally things Hunter sought from his family because, at the end of the day, he'd had a happy childhood. His trauma came much later.

"Thanks," Hunter said, looking his father in the eye.

"Let's go through my closet. You know your mother—she'll want you looking like a prince," Mark said, a smile on his face.

26

———

CHAPTER TWENTY-SIX.

The traditional black tuxedo was ignored, left hanging in a zipped-up bag in the back of his parents' second closet. Hunter fidgeted with a pin on his lapel. The fabric, the darkest of green, highlighted the gold vine-shaped trinket that gleamed in the light of the natural flame in their living room fireplace.

"I know you think you're some kind of dork and all," Mark told him upstairs, "but you're my son, and we are handsome devils."

Mark wasn't wrong; Hunter's skin was smooth, shaved, his hair textured and pushed back with some product, curling at the ends. A black button-up shirt lay under his jacket, highlighting the blue in his eyes.

The catering staff had begun to set up in the family kitchen for tomorrow's holiday. Based on the number of crates brought in, Hunter assumed a too-large party was being deliberately left undiscussed around him.

Of course, Mother would want us home for something like that.

A symphony of cozy sounds filled the air: the crackle of the fireplace, chopping from the kitchen, and soft Christmas music playing from a vintage radio across the room on the chestnut armoire.

"It's getting late." Hunter checked his gold watch. I should call. We'll be leaving anytime now, and they haven't even checked in."

It was just past 7:30 pm, and the ball started in half an hour.

"Oh, you know women," Mark said as one of the caterers walked into the room with two glasses of spiced eggnog. Mark's eyes lit up as he took both glasses, handing one to Hunter. "What's the rush anyway?"

"If we get there on time, we can come back earlier." Hunter shrugged, sipping the thick liquid and grimacing. "That is strong."

It started faint, a new noise that grew into a crescendo, separating itself from the calming background noise. A calamity of the unmistakable sound of heels skittering across the floor, coming closer to them.

"Your mother's home."

Hunter turned, straining to hear another set of footsteps, but there was undoubtedly only one pair of feet hurrying towards them.

"Something is wrong," Hunter said out loud. Mark's eyebrows rose, his attention shifting to look for his wife's face to appear in the entrance to the living room. When she did appear, her blonde hair was more frizzy than he had seen in a while, her breath was fast, and her pupils were large.

"Where's Olivia?" It was the only thing Hunter could think about, waiting for her to be safely back in his arms.

"What's wrong, dear?" Mark asked, walking towards her.

Where is Olivia?

"What's wrong?" Minerva laughed. "What's wrong? We spent the entire day shopping and sitting at the salon, only for it to start raining. On top of that, we are running late. This is turning out to be a catastrophe."

Hunter's shoulders relaxed a little as he sensed no immediate danger other than his mother's arms flying around as she gesticulated like an actress in a classic black and white movie.

"Yes, we should be going," Hunter said, setting his drink down. "Is Olivia already in the car?"

"Oh, my heavens, there are so many things wrong with that sentence," Minerva huffed.

"Wrong?"

His mother was impossible.

"Yes. One, we have to give a lady her proper grand reveal. Two, I have a driver waiting for you. You cannot take her to a formal outing in your beat-up old vehicle."

"Dad's truck is older than my car . . ." Hunter mumbled.

"Hey, it's a Tacoma. It holds its value."

"Shall we?" Minerva pushed the two men out of the living room. "I made Olivia go upstairs to wait for us."

"Why is she upstairs?" Hunter shook his head. "It makes zero sense."

"How else is she supposed to have a grand reveal? All that work we did today is not going to waste. I will ensure that she gets her movie moment. You'll never believe this, Mark—oh Hunter, I'm sure you already know—Olivia has never been to a prom. Poor thing, she barely even seemed to grasp the idea of high school. She seems pretty sheltered from the real world."

"It sounds like you two bonded," Hunter said, walking out to the foyer where the large staircase with wooden beams awaited—where his heartbeat stopped, where he forgot how to breathe, where he saw Olivia for the first time since the morning.

She was absolutely devastating, standing at the top of the stairs, looking down at them with a shy smile. 'Butterflies in his stomach' was too weak a phrase for how Hunter felt when those beautiful, dark green eyes connected with his, when his soul wanted to jump out of his body and connect with hers.

Looking up at Olivia, he knew she was destiny. There was no other way to describe it. She was home.

"Come on down, dear," Minerva said.

Olivia obeyed, her hand on the railing, her bright red nails gleaming against the wood as she stepped down slowly, traveling toward Hunter, their bodies waiting to reunite as electricity filled the air.

His father grunted uncomfortably. "Well, that's a pretty black dress," Mark said as Olivia reached the bottom of the steps. Hunter reached out toward her, their hands touching. Relief flooded him, to be back together and touch her again. How could he ever let go again now?

"Pretty black dress? Your words don't do her any justice," Minerva said, frowning, clearly disappointed. "She is one of the most stunning women I've ever seen in one of the most breathtaking dresses I've ever purchased."

Olivia stepped into the room like midnight incarnate, the sweeping train of her gown trailing behind her like spilled ink across marble. Layers of sheer tulle fluttered with each breath of air, catching the dim light and casting it back in glimmers that danced like dying embers. The bodice clung to her like a vow, sculpted and boned, corseted with devotion and secrets, while lace, black as a raven's wing, crawled delicately over her skin like a lover's touch.

It wasn't just a dress. It was a spell. A declaration. Her song in physical form.

Hunter wanted to fall to his knees, willing to burn in hell for a chance to undo the buttons down her spine.

His mother was right; it was much more than a pretty black dress.

There was a touch more magic: some blush on her skin, some sparkles on her eyelids, and a lip color that was not quite red but also not quite purple, making her eyes dance alive like embers in a fire.

"First of all, her long hair took ninety minutes to get a proper blowout. Don't you love how the ends wisp up, like she's Farrah Fawcett?" Minerva explained their day.

"How are you?" Hunter asked in a hushed voice, trying to pretend to listen to his mother's ranting. "I missed you so much."

Olivia intertwined her fingers with his and brushed her lips on the back of his hand, letting her tongue linger there, a private moment that couldn't be seen as anything more than innocent affection from his parent's angle.

"Oh, Hunter, you're in a green suit. I knew we should have gone for red, Olivia, to keep on the Christmas spirit theme."

"She's perfect, Mother," Hunter said. "Let's see this car waiting outside for us."

Minerva fussed over Olivia's skirt. "There, now she's perfect." She gave Olivia a half-hug. "You have fun, my dear."

The two walked out of the house, and a black Range Rover was waiting for them. The exhaust steamed up into the sky, fading into the red hue from the illuminated tail lights, and the SUV shifted as the driver put it into park, then jumped out to open the doors for them.

"Thank you for working on a holiday," Hunter said to the man, who smiled politely but mostly kept his head down.

Olivia sat as Hunter moved to the other side of the car so she didn't have to scoot. Once seatbelts were on, the car was in motion. The sun was officially down, and light rain pattered on the windows as dots of water pooled onto the glass, hitting one another and swallowing smaller beads whole.

"Are you excited?" Hunter asked Olivia, who seemed very lost in the darkness outside her window, her hands wrapped around her waist as she hugged herself. "What are you thinking about?"

"The world in the light," Olivia replied, "is absurdly ugly.

Don't you think so?" She finally tore her eyes away from her view, connecting back with him.

"You might be one of the few people with that belief." Hunter smiled. "I love it. I love the way you think."

"The dark—it's a blanket, an embrace. It soothes me. I feel safer."

"Will you be okay there at the ball?" Hunter asked.

Olivia's eyes seem to widen. "Will you?"

Hunter's stomach sank. He wasn't expecting that; he wasn't expecting her to protect him from his own heart, his own self.

"Will I ever fully be yours if I live in Sarah's shadow? In her darkness?"

He paused, not knowing if he could give the right answer. "The person I was with Sarah is not the same person I am now, Olivia."

"Perhaps it's best if we stay in the darkness," Olivia said. "The light can make us so ugly. Will you sing for me, Hunter?"

It was as if he could hear a symphony around him: the soft strokes of a piano key in his head, the sad, sweet notes of a violin. The back of the car, waiting for him like it was magic.

Is this what you hear, Olivia?

"If I say no, would you make me anyway?"

He had to know. He had to see that he was here, his free will intact, that it wasn't all a spell, a haze that he had convinced himself of breaking.

"If I feel helpless, I will protect myself," Olivia promised.

"Do you feel helpless now?"

"I feel safe with you, Hunter. You and the darkness are one, wrapped around me."

Hunter nodded. It was answer enough.

"I feel the same," Hunter said. "I can hear music."

"Can you still hear it?" Olivia's eyebrows raised.

Hunter nodded; he could.

"I hear it," she said. "I hear it always. It's the Earth; it always sings."

With a deep breath, even though everything in his social conditioning resisted it, Hunter opened his mouth, found the notes in his chest, and let them out.

"Your song is a curse that I wear like a crown
And I'd fall through your hell just to not let you drown
You bloom in the dark, where no garden should grow
But I'll drink of your thorns and I'll never let go."

"I've never heard that song before," Olivia said, smiling. "Sing more."

"Come back to me, my siren, my moon
My silver-bell song, my haunted desire
You breathe like the forest; you break like the sea
But I'll be the storm if it brings you to me
Come back to me, come back to me
My siren."

"It's about me?" Olivia breathed.

"My life, Olivia, is now about you."

"You called me a siren again," she said. "I can't say that I have ever tried to swim."

Olivia leaned in to Hunter, and her lips touched his. The heat in the car seemed to soar, and his heart beat like he was running in a race, the finish line just ahead with promises of uncertainty, only the beauty of the moon in his view.

"We are here," the driver announced as the car drew to a stop. Hunter could see the large brick estate lit up spectacularly out the tinted windows. People dressed in their winter formal best walked up the steps, exiting their own luxury vehicles. Carolers waited at the top of the steps, humming together in tune to a medley of holiday songs.

Hunter ran around the car to Olivia, the driver already there, holding an umbrella over her head as rain continued to dust the air around them.

"I've got it," Hunter said, taking the umbrella, letting him know his job was done.

Together, they took in the ten-foot wreaths hanging from the roof and the greens, golds, and reds across the front of the building.

"They certainly put on a show," Hunter said, turning to Olivia, whose face had fallen. "What's wrong?"

"Hunter, you once said that a siren is a witch."

27

———

CHAPTER TWENTY-SEVEN.

onfused, Hunter cocked his head, but he didn't get a chance to answer as a man in a coat and top hat ushered them inside, taking their tickets and displaying the biggest smile.

"Let's get your lady out of this mist. Enjoy yourselves."

Olivia wrapped her arm around Hunter, holding her skirt up with her other hand. It struck Hunter for the first time how it looked like she really belonged there. The elegance of the way she walked was like a ballet dancer sashaying across lily pads. The certainty of how she held herself was that of a person who'd had power her entire life, but it was normal, unremarkable to her. Everything that this ball was trying to be, the holiday magic so forced, was everything that Olivia truly was.

This ball didn't deserve her.

They moved through the grand foyer, where a large Christmas tree sat in the middle of the room to greet them, and a line for the open bar wrapped partially around it as gentlemen in black coats waited to bring champagne flutes to their dates.

"You're upset," Hunter said.

Olivia was too quiet. The energy that radiated off of her was tense, despite the slight dimples in her cheeks as she smiled and ignored his words. That smile did not meet her eyes.

His alarm bells were going off as he studied her face, her mouth neutral, her head hanging high as she scanned the room.

"Is it the tree?" Hunter asked.

Olivia shook her head.

Flickering candles lined the end tables of the room, shadows striking against the bells and holly lining the walls in draped greenery—a classic holiday look. Hunter felt his throat tighten, nervous, sensitive to every look, every twitch of Olivia's nose.

This was once her home.

Maybe this was too soon.

"I'm sorry," Hunter said. "We shouldn't be here, should we?"

A trance seemed to fall over her, Olivia's voice a higher pitch than her normal tone.

"No songs tonight, do you think you can make it? We can turn around right now," Hunter said, gripping her hand tighter. "Whatever you need, I will make it so."

A small smile played across her lips at that. She turned her chin up to him. "There are no Danishes here, I'm afraid."

Hunter laughed and pulled her entirely into him, hugging her.

"Excuse you two, the foyer is not for standing around," an elderly woman bumped into them. "Get into the dance hall; go on now."

Olivia giggled and picked up her skirt, floating across the floor on Hunter's arm as they proceeded forward.

"I want to be here," she said.

The dance hall looked just as Hunter had seen it so many times between the field trips and the wedding. This time, it was filled with couples attempting to waltz, some beautiful dancers, others struggling. The ceilings were over twenty feet high, and dancers floated across a marble floor that seemed to trap any color or light that hit it.

He had been so focused on Olivia that he hadn't stopped to think of what seeing this room during an event might do to him, as he saw the ghost of Sarah swaying back and forth in her white princess gown, laughing and begging him to dance.

I've said goodbye.

He pushed the guilt down, though it wouldn't leave properly. He adjusted the band of his watch uncomfortably.

"This is where it happened," Olivia whispered to him.

Indeed, it was, for both of them.

"I cannot promise I won't step on your feet," Hunter said, offering his hand with a crooked, self-deprecating smile. "But I feel it's my solemn duty to ask you to dance."

Olivia tilted her head, gaze shimmering with mischief beneath the candlelight. "A duty? My, how terribly noble. Tell me, Mr. Gunnan, do you often offer yourself as tribute to ballroom casualties?"

He smirked, bowing slightly. "Only to the most dangerous women."

"Then you ought to be more careful," she said, placing her hand in his. "I've been known to leave a mark."

As he guided her onto the floor, she moved like mist, graceful, impossible to hold. "You dance like someone with something to prove," she said, eyes twinkling as she floated beside him.

"I probably do," he murmured. "I haven't done this since the wedding, and before that, when Mother pushed me into ballroom lessons when I was a teen. How about yourself?"

"Oh, I dance to keep the ghosts in their place," she replied lightly, though her gaze flicked toward the grand chandelier as if watching something invisible sway above them. "They tend to grow bold when the violins begin."

Hunter studied her face, his grin fading. "You alright?"

She gave a small smile, too perfect to be real. "Do I appear otherwise?"

"You're quiet. Even for you."

Her gaze drifted over the polished floors, the gilded crown molding, the shadows cast by flickering candlelight. "This room is a mirror. It remembers things I'd rather not see."

"Then let's leave," he said immediately. "We can leave now."

Olivia turned to him slowly, her voice a murmur, almost a laugh. "And miss all the fun? I've grown rather fond of my ghosts, you know. We've shared so many seasons together."

Hunter's grip on her waist tightened slightly. "You shouldn't have to keep them company."

She looked up at him then, and for a moment, her mask slipped. "At least ghosts answer back."

He stopped moving. The room spun gently without them.

"Talk to me," he said. "Don't make me guess."

Her lips curved into a soft, strange smile. "Isn't it a bit romantic, though? All this glitter and memory. The illusion of joy stitched over something broken. Like lace over a wound."

"Don't do that," Hunter said, voice low. "Don't make it poetry so that it hurts less."

Her chin lifted. "I wasn't. Some things are beautiful because they hurt."

Hunter brushed a gloved thumb along her cheek, steady and tender. "You don't have to carry it alone."

For a breath, she just looked at him—like he was something wild she didn't know how to hold. Then, quietly, "You don't know what it is to be from a place that loved you once, and looks right through you now."

"Then tell me," he said. "Make me see you."

Olivia's voice softened, formal and haunting. "This room watched me become someone I no longer recognized. I stood here in silk and silence while everything I loved unravelled beneath crystal chandeliers. And unfortunately, everyone noticed."

He stepped closer. "Is it better if they didn't?"

Her eyes glistened, but she blinked the tears back like a lady taught never to let emotion show. "I think I'd like to stay, just a little while longer. I want to see if the ghosts remember me."

Hunter wrapped her in his arms and began to sway, ignoring the tempo of the music entirely. "Then we'll stay. And if they do, let them know you're not alone anymore."

Counting his steps in his head, Hunter spun Olivia, her dress fanning out around her as colors combined, the other dancers and their gowns twirling to the same choreography. He was keeping up well. There were no moments of pain or stumbling. Olivia fit in like she was born to be here.

That's because she was.

They moved to music that was really there, that wasn't in his head. He appreciated that, seeing the eight-piece orchestra, the violinists who played with their entire bodies, dressed in black as if they were supposed to fade into the walls but instead showed up to be noticed.

The music was fast and lively—magic, a twinkle in the energy, in the air, as a large grand clock ticked, filling the room with natural percussion counting down until midnight.

Until Christmas.

Smiles lingered on faces, and cups clanged together in toasts as groups celebrated. A whirl of joy surrounded them like dust from a faerie sprinkled over their heads. Hunter felt lighter, more in control, as he breathed in Olivia's scent. Her skin, her neck, and her lips were inches from his face at all times.

He wanted to freeze time, to live in a moment of bliss where Olivia smiled, secrets hidden behind those eyes, secrets for him to discover, to obsess over. This would be short-lived; their world crashing down as the reality of their pain overwhelmed both of them. Hunter could see him running out of there as Sarah crept into the back of his mind. The last time he'd danced with a woman here was when she was in his arms.

How do I disappear into you? Hunter thought, as Olivia's eye bore into him.

She saw him, like no one else did. She saw his pain in a different light, not as someone who needed help or saving, but as a companion. Both of them existed in a haunted sadness that would never be lifted, except for the comfort of each other's arms.

The music slowed and came to an end, the ballroom breaking out in applause and appreciation as the band announced a small break and waiters came through with small hors d'oeuvres and champagne in small, stemmed circular glasses.

Olivia didn't let Hunter look away from her, their bodies not breaking from their dance as everyone moved more casually around them, a few awkward stares thrown in their direction.

"Hunter." Her face, the quiver of her lip, told him all he needed to know about where her heart lived. "The last time I was in this ballroom, I was called the worst possible thing imaginable. A boy who held me close, who said the most beautiful words to me, called me a witch. You called me a siren. It is the same, isn't it?"

It hurt her, that word.

It shouldn't hurt, Olivia. I don't want it to hurt.

"But Olivia," Hunter said, his hands slipping down to her waist, pulling her into him, into their bubble hidden from the world, "you *are* a witch."

She pushed herself away so fast, tears filling her eyes instantly.

"No, stop." He grabbed her hand before she could turn, her body poised to run. She stilled, as he asked.

"You didn't let me finish."

"I didn't think you could hurt me. I thought you were different, Hunter."

"Olivia, you are a witch. And I'm so proud of you," he breathed.

"What?"

"I am so proud of everything you are. You can be terrifying, sure, but who isn't sometimes? You are the strongest person I've ever met, you are sure of yourself, you are more beautiful than any forest, than any moon, mother nature bows down at your feet because she cannot compare to your beauty, she cannot compare to the compassion you hold in your heart."

"I want them all dead," Olivia said. "Everyone who walks on two legs and shares a tongue like mine. How is that for compassion? You are proud of me, of this evil being that I am, of this horror."

Hunter put his hand under her chin. "Stop, Olivia. It isn't 1914. Everything you are and everything you want to be is something that I love. I love you."

She did stop. The slight angling away from him, the pull of her body against him, ceased. There was a limpness in her, as if she were about to faint into him.

It would be okay if she did. He would hold her, carry her forever.

"Who could ever love a witch, Hunter? What does that say about you?"

"I don't care what anyone says. Because you could do nothing to scare me away, there is nothing you can do to make me feel differently. I am here with you in this ballroom, in this place filled with the ghosts you speak of, my own ghosts, because you wanted to stay. I will always stay."

"Let myself be a witch, then? That's what I should do? And then say it back, say that I love you?"

"I would never tell you what to say," Hunter said.

Olivia's chest rose and fell as she breathed, staring at him silently, thinking, contemplating.

"I don't belong in this world, Hunter."

"I know." He nodded.

"You don't belong here either."

"No?"

"No. That's why your song woke me up. That's why you heard the music." Olivia stepped back, her heel hitting the marble with a new intent. Her hand lingered on his as she grabbed him, tugging, asking.

"Come with me," she whispered, but it was loud enough for him to understand, to grab hold of unspoken promises, of seduction under holiday decor and a grandiose display of wealth.

"Where?" he asked, clearing his throat. "Where do you want to go?"

"Away, Hunter. I've always just wanted to take you away. Say yes."

"I'm yours. However, you need me. However you'll have me."

She looked at him as if that was not answer enough, or she was unsure.

"Let me clarify," he continued. "Yes."

It's all she seemed to be waiting to hear—her breath caught in the space between them, eyes wide like a flame had just been lit behind them. Then her body was moving, reaching for him as though the ache of distance had been unbearable, as though it were possible for them to become one soul in two skins. Her hands found the sides of his face, velvet-gloved and trembling slightly as she hummed, and her scent changed to something sweet, something toxic.

It didn't come shyly, nor gently. Olivia kissed him like a woman desperate to memorize his taste before time pulled them apart. And he kissed her back just as fiercely, as though the shape of her mouth was the only true thing he'd ever known. Their lips moved like they had something to say that couldn't be told in words. As if life itself hung in the balance of that moment—hungry, breathless, full of everything they had never dared admit.

The world around them softened. The sounds of laughter and music dulled to a hush, like someone had placed thick velvet over the whole ballroom. The candles flickered taller. The air thickened.

When they finally pulled apart, their foreheads resting against each other's, Hunter shivered.

Not from cold—but from something deeper, stranger. A chill that bloomed inside his ribs and radiated outward, like a snowfall beginning in his lungs. His fingers tightened instinctively around the band of his watch. The metal felt too warm, too still.

Something is off.

The feeling wasn't fear exactly—it was wonder laced with disquiet. The sense that they weren't entirely real anymore. That they were simply figures inside a snowglobe someone had shaken too hard—spinning, swirling, trapped in perfect motion. The storm outside still howled against the windows, but the droplets never touched the glass.

Time hadn't just slowed.

It had stopped.

And in that eerie stillness, something inside him whispered: *Remember this. This is the last time you'll ever feel the world breathing.*

Olivia pulled back just enough to look at him. Her eyes were wet, shining with something that looked too big to name.

"It's calling. Can you hear it?" she whispered.

Hunter could.

28

CHAPTER TWENTY-EIGHT.

There was music again—ethereal and faerie-like, a call, a promise, a broken heart. The band was there, setting back up as they prepared for their next set, but they were not playing.

"You'll hear it always, the song," Olivia promised. "The Earth, it's all around us. Calling me, calling us."

A man stopped in his tracks, staring at Olivia in disbelief. "Will you save a dance for me?"

"I'm spoken for," she said. He shrugged and walked away.

Olivia held out her hand for Hunter to grab, and he obliged. It was unbelievable that anyone here wouldn't already know that he was hers. He felt his chest puff out, his posture straighten, like a peacock presenting to keep other suitors away.

Her hand in his was soft, and she gripped him hard. Her touch always felt good, but now it was a new type of euphoria, a glittery new drug running through his bloodstream. The snowglobe effect around him made the lights glow a little brighter, and the greens especially were more pigmented. Everything else, though, had become extremely displeasing, nearly hurting his eyes.

Electricity seemed to hum, a loud buzzing in his ear like a fly that wouldn't leave him alone. Furniture that would be considered handsome—sofas, tables, and chairs, seemed victimized—like dead bodies fallen where no one could hear them scream.

The marble floor, which moments ago was shiny and gleaming, was now a portal threatening to open up and swallow him whole.

But Olivia stroked his cheek, bringing his focus back to her, and it felt so good, too good, like he was now in a dream, and her touch would convince him to never wake up.

"What did you do?" Hunter asked.

"You said yes," she said, before pulling him forward, walking him out of the ballroom and back through the foyer where the Christmas tree had so much life, so much passion— so much beauty that felt like he was in the presence of God. Tears pooled in his eyes.

"Yes to what?"

"To being free."

The humming, the electricity, the music that no one else heard—it was all still moving around him, caressing him, whispering to him, seducing him.

Olivia kept her eyes forward, guiding him away, not stopping as eyes in the room darted to her, the maiden who was practically running for the door.

The loud crashing sound of the grandfather clock flowed through Hunter's body, the vibrations in the floor moving up through his feet, his knees, as others around them toasted to the stroke of midnight.

Merry Christmas.

"Whoa, whoa there!" The door attendant laughed. "We

don't give refunds for lost glass slippers. Where are you off to so quickly?"

It was hard to tell with the music around him, with every heartbeat adding to the beat and rhythm that serenaded his soul, but Hunter heard discordant voices and screams behind him. His head was light, and it was hard to look back, like looking to the past was no longer something he would ever be capable of—as if he really had been set free.

Olivia ignored the man, pulling Hunter down the walkway. Instead of going to the parking lot, her heels hit sleet and snow over grass as they turned the corner, marching over the picnic area and straight toward the forest.

Hunter's vision was still affected, and now that he saw only nature in his view, he wondered if anyone had ever seen a beauty like this before. The white on the ground, the frost and the ice that dripped off of bushes that marked their path—all of it was a ghostly transparent diamond light, filling what should be darkness, a disco ball of sparkles and joy, a shaken snow globe where he was the nutcracker inside watching a world of wonder.

"The world is new." Hunter stopped moving, taking it all in.

His heightened sense of touch was overwhelming. He responded to Olivia's pull against him in the way a wolf would react to a bunny—carnal, wanting, needing.

Everything in his world was a sensation; everything in the world rang true with life.

The music swept him off his feet, begging him to waltz.

The trees in the distance called out to him. They sang, begging him to submit to a dance before he walked out into the night with his haunting love.

"Forever," he said. "My body is saying forever."

"It will always be like this," Olivia said. "I'm happy you like it. I'm happy that you can be a part of me now."

"Now?" Hunter asked. "Olivia, what did you do?"

"I made it so you can be with me forever," she said, tugging on his arm again, pulling him further until he stepped under trees, until he was in her home.

Our home.

With his back foot still on the covered grass, the last part of him not to be engulfed by thick trees, he paused. "Why do I feel like if I come with you, I'll never come out?"

Olivia turned to face him, her eyes so loving and light despite their dark pigment, like a disco of lights illuminating what he should not be able to see.

"We are never going back," she whispered. "You'll be with me forever. Even if you change your mind."

They moved through the trees as if the forest had been waiting for them—branches arching overhead like cathedral ceilings. Snowflakes drifted in soft spirals, catching in Olivia's dark curls like diamonds.

She led him with quiet certainty, barefoot now, her shoes forgotten against tree trunks behind them. Her dress tore, caught on branches, leaving behind a trail of their final decisions together.

The deeper they went, the quieter the world became. Even the sound of wind disappeared, the music faded, and the trees no longer spoke or sang.

"Where are we going?" Hunter asked. His voice sounded fainter than before. His breath barely clouded the air.

She didn't answer—not with words.

Olivia turned and looked at him with a kind of sorrowful tenderness he'd never seen before. Her hand found his cheek. She stroked it gently, as if memorizing the curve of his face.

And that was when he knew.

The chill in his bones. The too-still air. The snow that didn't melt on his skin.

Hunter wasn't alive anymore.

He staggered back a step. "Olivia."

"They discovered your body, fallen on the marble floor. Your parents, your friends, will have closure." Her voice cracked like a dried leaf. "I couldn't bear another Christmas alone."

He tried to speak—he should've been angry, should've shouted, should've run—but all that came was a broken breath.

And then she was in his arms again, curling into him like a ribbon folding in on itself.

"I'm sorry," she whispered into his coat. "I did it softly. You didn't feel a thing. I waited until you were happy."

He closed his eyes.

It was the kiss. Her taste had been different—her lips, poisonous like holly.

And when he opened them again, he understood: he *was* happy. The pain was gone. The fear. The weight of everything he'd ever lost. It was all gone.

What remained was *her.*

She led him to the oldest tree in the glade—tall as a bell tower, its bark glistening silver in the moonlight. Hollowed at the center, like a cradle for something precious and sacred.

Inside, soft moss grew in blankets. The tree hummed quietly, alive and ancient.

"It was the only option. I wouldn't have been able to stop you from aging, even if wrapped in the tree with me. Now your ghost belongs to a witch."

"To a siren. My moon, my tree siren," he corrected her.

Olivia looked up at him, her eyes bright and unrepentant. "Lie with me. Let this be our cathedral. Let the forest keep us."

Hunter hesitated for only a moment.

Then he wrapped his arms around her and let her pull him down into the tree's hollow. Her body curled against his like a final stanza. The moss rose around them like a blanket. Their hands twined together. His lips touched her hair.

"I forgive you," he murmured.

And her reply came soft and sharp as the falling snow. "I'd do it again."

The tree closed around them like the world was exhaling. Above them, the wind stirred through the branches, carrying the distant echo of ballroom music and the faint, dreamlike call of sirens.

"I'll be haunting you for the rest of eternity," Hunter promised.

"The tree siren and her phantom," Olivia mused.

"That has a certain ring."

"Good," Olivia said. "Because you'd better.'

Olivia started their forever with a song, her song.

Our song.

"Hark how the bells

Sweet silver bells

All seem to say

Throw cares away

Christmas is here, bringing good cheer."

"Goodbye," Hunter said out loud, as he shut out the memories of the world that had hurt him and buried himself in her arms for eternity.

HE COULD HEAR the children play as the years passed, as the school visited the grounds for field trips. Rumors of the spirits that lived in the forest were alive and well, helped by Sadie spreading stories that someone she knew had been murdered, and the witch had run into the night, the forest keeping her still, wrapped in evergreen and snowfall, tucked beneath the boughs like ornaments long forgotten. And every Christmas Eve, the wind carried music through the trees when the snow fell just right.

A waltz.

A laugh.

A kiss.

A song.

And the world, if only for a breath, remembered what it meant to be truly, hopelessly, joyfully in love. Hunter stayed forever wrapped in her safety, in her comfort—singing the songs for the trees, for the moon, for Olivia.

ALSO BY ELLE KAELEE

Dark Fantasy:

Glass Wings

Burning Glass

Glass Shadow

~

Gothic and Paranormal Romance:

Sweet Silver Bells

~

Stay Updated. Lots of future projects to come:

Visit ElleKaelee.com

ACKNOWLEDGMENTS

A novel is far from a solo project. Thank you to the following who helped my first romance come to life:

Developmental editing by Dan Hanks

Copy/line editing by Taylor Robinson

Beta readers: Stephanie Storm, Maggie Hoopis, Blair Asbury

Olivia character art by Jacquebrianne.com www.jacquebrianne.com

Cover illustrations and design by Kim Cavrak, spiritofebullience.com